NOWHERE LAND

DAVID L MARSDEN

authorHOUSE®

AuthorHouse™
1663 Liberty Drive
Bloomington, IN 47403
www.authorhouse.com
Phone: 1-800-839-8640

First published by AuthorHouse 6/22/2009

ISBN: 978-1-4389-8972-3 (sc)

Printed in the United States of America
Bloomington, Indiana

This book is printed on acid-free paper.

I Dedicate This Book To:
Pam Mc Kinney
Mary Ellison
Kathy Weiss
And my children

CONTENTS

Introduction   *In the Beginning*   ix

Chapter One   *King Addictions Takes Root*   1
                   A Visit to the Village Of Honesty   3

Chapter Two   *William Learns His Destiny*   6

Chapter Three   *William Meets Truth*   11
                   The Fall of King Nobody   13

Chapter Four   *William's Journey Begins*   15

Chapter Five   *King Addictions Rejoices*   20

Chapter Six   *Danielle Meets Denial*   23

Chapter Seven   *Denial Shows His Face*   25

Chapter Eight   *Negativity is Angered*   28

Chapter Nine   *A Meeting of the Positive Beings*   31

Chapter Ten   *The Sea of Confusion*   33

Chapter Eleven   *William and Danielle Meet the Keeper
                   of the Strait*   36

Chapter Twelve   *Zom Comes Aboard the Ship*   40

Chapter Thirteen   *King Addictions' Revenge*   44

Chapter Fourteen   *Deceit Does His Dirty Work*   47

Chapter Fifteen   *The People of the Deep*   50

Chapter Sixteen   *Deceit Returns to Finish the Job*   54

Chapter Seventeen   *William and Zom Reach the City
of Serenity*   57

Chapter Eighteen   *The Town Hall Meeting*   61
William, Zom Meet Vola and the Old One   61
*Entering the Cave and Beginning
the Journey*   65

Chapter Nineteen   *The Village of Backwards*   67

Chapter Twenty   *The Village of Backwards Summons
the Wizard*   71

Chapter Twenty-One   *Beginning the Journey Up the Mountain*   76
The Encounter with the Man in The Rut   77

Chapter Twenty-Two   *Danielle's Trial*   80

Chapter Twenty-Three   *William and His Friends Approach
the Castle of Addictions*   85

Chapter Twenty-Four   *William Battles Fear*   88

Chapter Twenty-Five   *Zom Meets Ignorance*   94

Chapter Twenty-Six   *The Battle with Addictions*   97

Chapter Twenty-Seven   *The Land of Nowhere Returns to the Light*   104
Danny's Soul Returns to His Body.   105

Chapter Twenty-Eight   *Positivity Battles Negativity*   107

Epilogue   111

INTRODUCTION

IN THE BEGINNING

The steady beep…beep…beep of the heart monitor filled the hospital room as the nurse checked the I.V. attached to her young patient. His pulse was steady – blood pressure good.

"Now, all you have to do is open those eyes," she whispered to the boy. She hated this ward. The staff called it the "place of the living dead" .It was filled with coma patients. Coma – what a depressing word, especially when it applied to a child like the boy Betty was now treating. She sighed and focused on the task at hand not noticing the old woman as she entered the room.

"New patient?"

Betty jumped at the sound of the woman's voice.

"Aggie, you scared me to death!"

She smiled at the old woman as she jotted down some notes on the boy's medical chart and placed it beside his bed.

"Yes. He came in two days ago. We haven't been able to identify him yet. We think he's homeless."

"Drugs," said Aggie, as she stood staring with no emotion showing on her deeply-lined face.

"Maybe you can work your magic with him Aggie." The young nurse said.

She peered out the door towards the nurses' station.

"My replacement is here. I'll see you next week, okay?" There was no response from the old woman. As Betty left the room, Aggie took a seat in the chair next to the bed and took the boy's hand in hers.

Betty greeted her replacement with a look of surprise.

"Sara, what are *you* doing here? Where is Julie?"

"Oh, we swapped so she could have a long weekend." Her colleague replied, as she swept her long, blonde hair up into a bun and placed her cap over it.

"Who's the little old lady?"

"Oh, she comes in every Friday night and reads and talks to the coma patients. Her name is Aggie.She's kind of a fortune-teller." Betty explained, noting her friend's reaction.

"Really?" Sara whispered.

"Is she any good?

Has she ever told you *your future*?"

Betty laughed. "No way. I don't want to know about that."

She grabbed her purse and started heading down the hospital corridor.

"Today's notes are on the counter. Have fun." She said, as she was going out the door.

"Yeah." Sara waved to her co-worker and walked into the room towards the boy.The old woman didn't acknowledge her.There was something strange about her that Sara couldn't pinpoint.

She was a small woman and appeared to be about seventy years old. She was nicely dressed and her gray hair was pinned neatly on top of her head in a bun.

Sara cleared her throat."My name is Sara.

I'm the nurse on duty tonight."

Aggie turned her gaze upon the nurse.

"I…I just want to say, I think it's great that you take your time to come here for the patients." For some reason Aggies eyes un-nerved Sara. They were friendly yet mysteriously hypnotic.

Aggie looked away, breaking the trance and focused back upon the sleeping youth." This one is special." She thought to herself.

"So." "Do you know him?" Sara asked.

"No." Aggie replied.

"Well, we call him Johnny for John Doe."

"His name is Danny," Aggie interrupted. "His parents both died from drug and alcohol abuse, and he's been on the streets since he was twelve."

Sara stared at her in amazement.

"I thought you said you didn't know him?"

"I don't, child." Aggie replied.

"Well. I…I had better make my rounds," Sara said, feeling a sudden urge to get away from this strange woman.

Aggie waited for Sara to leave the room. Then she placed her hands over Danny's hands and put her mouth up to his ear.

"Can you hear me, Danny? You will be fine." She whispered.

"You will awaken from your sleep a stronger person, and you will lead many others to better places in their lives."

She sat back and folded her hands in her lap.

"I have a story to tell you, Danny. And I want you to listen very carefully."She paused for a moment as if waiting for a response. "The story is called "Nowhere Land", and it's about a place you already know very well."

Then she began.

CHAPTER ONE

KING ADDICTIONS TAKES ROOT

D own...down...down...went the soul of Danny. As his soul fell further and further into the dark abyss called death, pictures of his life appeared before him -pictures of all the times he could have said no to alcohol and drugs but gave in to the temptation to use instead.

Out of the stillness a voice roared loudly." You are going to die. You are going to die."Suddenly, another voice came out from the darkness, and it was Aggies voice. "No! The boy will not die. Instead, he will learn about the weapons called Alcohol and Drugs."

And, from the darkness, came a bright white light that encircled Danny. The light then transported him to another world called the Land of Nowhere.

"Listen to me now, Danny, because it may be you're last chance," spoke Aggie.

Danny's soul ended up landing on top of a hill under a blue sky on a sunny day. Danny felt at ease for the first time in a long time.

"I will listen to anything you have to say, if it will help me!" exclaimed Danny.

"I am tired of being sick and afraid all of the time and even more afraid to die," continued Danny.

"Good!" replied Aggie.

"Where are we?" asked Danny.

"We are in the Land of Nowhere, and this is where you will stay for awhile until you have learned some very important things," replied Aggie.

"I can't see my body!" exclaimed Danny in a trembling voice.

"You have no body.It is still fighting for life on a hospital bed in the other world!" exclaimed Aggie.

Aggie told Danny that he could travel in his soul and that he would follow a story about to take place in the Land of Nowhere.

She also told Danny that he must listen carefully and learn as much as possible about the story in order to save his life and his soul.

"I am listening," said Danny.

"Listen very closely because you're very soul depends upon it!" exclaimed Aggie.

Then she began the story.

Once upon a time, in a place that existed in the souls of humanity, there was a land that was named, and rightfully so, I might add, "The Land of Nowhere." In this land there ruled a king who thought of himself as a very wealthy and wise man, indeed. He was a tall, slender fellow with a white bristle beard and mustache. Although his light blue eyes held many happy memories of years past and that certain wisdom that only comes with age, his eyes could not conceal the lost expression upon his face. He very rarely smiled, because he was not aware of his own feelings, thus, living up to his name, King Nobody.

Nowhere Land, as the locals called it, had once been a lush and beautiful place with deep blue skies, crystal clear lakes and dark green grass that complimented the assorted flowers of the land. Lately, however, it was mysteriously growing ugly and dark. This world of theirs consisted of the land they lived on and the Dark Land on the other side of their ocean, but they dare not think about the Dark Land, for, it too, was once a lush paradise. Now, no vegetation grew on its lifeless soil, because it was becoming dark and barren. Dark clouds surrounded the land which was making true life almost non- existent. Even the once majestic ancient castle, with it's large towers and stained glass windows, was surrounded by dead trees and weeds which grew up its sides, as if the hands of the Devil himself was embracing it with his bony, withered fingers.In this castle there ruled a very different kind of King. His name was King Addictions. He was a hideous looking man who took on any number of different forms.He could actually change form, at will, to fit whatever situation may arise.He had many Knights in dark armor, and his favorites were constantly busy working for him in those dark days.

King Addictions' favorite Knights were Sir Denial, Sir Fear, and Sir Confusion. These Knights were the ones called upon the most to aid the Dark King in his handiwork. Only one other Knight did Addictions call on as often, and that was the most sinister of all - Sir Death.

As with most great Knights of the times, powerful weapons were bestowed upon them to use in battle, but these Knights did not need forged steel swords nor thick protective shields, my friend, for these weapons were not needed to do the Dark King's bidding. No. King Addictions' greatest weapons which were carried by each of his Knights were the most horrifying weapons of mass destruction ever created - Alcohol and Drugs. With these weapons, his Knights would travel over to the more beautiful part of their world and steal the souls of the people. They were not interested in the bodies of the people, only the souls.

When these souls were won over, they were placed in the hands of King Addictions. He would immediately throw them into the Sea of Confusion to wash away all feelings of hope. He knew if these souls were given even an ounce of hope, they could fight back against the weapons - Alcohol and Drugs, and could possibly be restored back into their bodies and return to their happy lives. When the lost souls were beyond all hope, he would then lock them in the dungeons on the lower level of his castle but allow their physical form to continue functioning freely. So, in a sense, these poor hollow people with no souls were still alive though their souls were held captive. People in this Dark State were never happy or playful. They could not see the beauty of the blue skies nor the crystal lakes and the green grass. Those who lost their souls to King Addictions knew nothing of good feelings such as happiness, peace, or contentment. When people were in this Dark State, they only felt the opposite of positive. They felt only negative.

A VISIT TO THE VILLAGE OF HONESTY

On a certain day in one of the many villages that existed in the Land of Nowhere, the Knight, Sir Denial, was sent from the Dark Land to do King Addictions' bidding. The task that Sir Denial was given was to attempt to alter an entire village from living truthfully.By bringing the people under his power, he could blind them from Honesty and Truth.

The name of the village was the Village of Honesty, and, until that certain day, all of the people in the village were happy and content with their way of life. However, the Knight, Sir Denial, wielded the powerful weapons - Alcohol and Drugs.

At the gate to the Village of Honesty there stood a guard named Barthold. He was a man of great height and weight.

Barthold, being over six feet nine inches tall and weighing three hundred pounds, did, indeed, keep the gate safe.

Barthold descended from a long line of gatekeepers. His father and grandfather before him were gatekeepers, and, like his forefathers, Barthold had dark curly hair and a bushy unkempt beard that grew up instead of down.In order for him to see, he had to comb his beard to the side of his face, making him look funny and seem as if he were a little crazy. His appearance only helped in putting fear into any traveler wishing to gain access to the village. Whenever a traveler would show up at the gate, the gatekeeper would bellow in a loud gruff voice, "Who wishes to gain entrance to this village?"

This, too, would make most travelers shake in fear, and, once the gatekeeper was sure they were fearful enough, he would soften up just a little - just a tiny bit, because the gatekeeper's job was to make sure only good, honest people entered the Village of Honesty. Henceforth, it was only good and honest people who did not have anything to fear. So, if they stood their ground and took the time to get to know the gatekeeper better, then, they passed the first entrance test. Once the travelers knew Barthold, they were no longer afraid of him. On the contrary, they found out that he was quite a nice fellow.After Barthold was sure the people wishing entrance to the village were honest people, he lowered his defenses and welcomed them into the village.

On this particular day, Barthold was unknowingly up against something that he was no match for. Sir Denial did not shake or run in fear of Barthold's looks or gruff voice. Instead, he approached the gate of the village asking to gain entrance.

"I am Sir Denial, and I have many delicious food stuffs which could benefit this village," he said.

The gatekeeper saw no dishonesty in the eyes of the traveler and asked the one question that every stranger wanting access into the Village of Honesty needed to answer before the gates were opened for him.

"Are you an honest person?" Barthold asked in his husky voice with great authority and a good hard stare. This was to let the stranger know that he meant business.

"Indeed, dear gatekeeper, I am truly an honest person," Sir Denial said, with a devious smile on his face. Of course, he was lying.

Barthold rubbed his beard for a minute and stared into the traveler's eyes before he replaced his harsh look with a bright smile that filled his eyes with merriment. He bid the stranger entrance to the village. However, before entering the village, Sir Denial bowed and said in a very friendly way. "Such kindness should be rewarded, dear gatekeeper." Sir Denial pulled a flask out of his ragged farmers garment and said, "Take ye this refreshing drink, and wet your whistle a bit, for you look thirsty, and I can see that you work very hard and deserve a fine drink."

The flask, of course, contained the weapon - Alcohol. Now, you may ask, "Why would an honest man like Barthold accept this deadly weapon?" Well, my friend, he had no reason not to trust Denial. After all, he lived in a village where honesty was a way of life, and he thought it rude not to accept this man's kindness, so he accepted and took several gulps.

Upon drinking, Barthold experienced an odd feeling. It was as if he had no cares in the world, and he liked it very much. A little voice inside of him bid him caution which, normally, he would have listened to immediately and stopped what he was doing - much like the time he was so hungry he wanted to leave his post at the gate, just for the teeniest minute, to get something to eat. The little cautious voice stopped him. He did the honorable and wise thing and stayed Barthold had been very proud of himself, as well he should have been.

But this was different. The little cautious voice didn't seem so right. "What could it possibly hurt to take just one more swig of this delightful drink?" something inside of him made him ask.

"Have you more of this remarkable drink?" asked Barthold.

"Of course," Denial replied.

He gave the gatekeeper more to drink, and, as he entered the gate, he laughed a very evil laugh and thought to himself, "How easy this task for King Addictions is going to be." Now, normally, Barthold would have noticed this evil laugh after all, an evil laugh can only come from a dishonest person. However, the weapon Alcohol was doing its job very well indeed, and, at that point, the gate keeper just didn't care.Not caring is the most destructive attitude a human can have, my friend. Because of poor, dear Barthold making that one bad decision, the demise of an unknowing and unfortunate village was about to begin.

CHAPTER TWO

WILLIAM LEARNS HIS DESTINY

In this Village of Honesty, there lived an honest boy known to the people of the village, as William. William had no family. His parents had been taken by the good Being Natural Death, (not to be mistaken for the sinister Sir Death). They were taken when William was very young. Natural Death was from the Good Realm, sent down by The Creator to gather a person's soul when the physical body could no longer function.Natural Death's job was to take the good soul up to The Creator, and the body, which was no longer or important, would then receive a proper burial. The souls who were taken by Natural Death were those that lived their lives helping others. Even if they had fallen to the Dark Side at times in their lives, they could turn their lives around to the good before it was too late.

The people of the Village Of Honesty that knew William and his family took pity on the boy and kept William in his own house of birth taking turns on different days raising the child. They made sure he was fed and clothed. But, most importantly of all, they made sure he was cared for emotionally. They nurtured him with love, understanding and kindness. Because of this, although William was poor, he was very happy and grateful.

He was in the middle of his fourteenth year of life and wore tattered hand-me-down clothes, but he did not care. William had a very big heart, which made him the richest boy in the village. His long red hair and big green eyes accented the pale freckles on his face. Despite his poverty, William remained happy and content with his life. He loved the people of his village as much as they loved him.

One day, when he was taking a break from the numerous chores he did for the village people, he sat on his favorite hill that overlooked the village. The sky was extremely blue that day, and, as William was marveling at how beautiful it was, he heard a voice, and it startled him.

"Who speaks too me?" he asked as he looked around to find the owner of this voice. Imagine his surprise when a cloud took the shape of a man. William blinked his eyes thinking that he was in the middle of a dream.

"Hear me!" the voice bellowed. The words appeared to be coming from the cloud, and William soon realized that he did not fear this unknown entity. On the contrary, as the words were spoken, William felt a cool, pleasant breeze that seemed to bathe him in goodness.

"You are a poor peasant boy, but, in the realm in which I exist, you are greatly exalted," spoke the cloud.

"Thank you." William's reply was whispered, and he wondered what he was doing sitting on the top of a hill talking to a cloud. He pinched himself to make sure he was awake. "Ouch. Yes, I am awake," he thought to himself.

"You are kind and loving and hold a strong faith in the positive things in your life!" the cloud spoke again.

"Who...Who are you?" William stuttered.

"I am one not bound by the laws of your world. I am one who has always been and, to you. I am your destiny," answered the cloud.

William scratched his head and was about to ask the cloud what the word "destiny" meant when the cloud spoke again. "You are the weapon chosen to defeat the forthcoming evil."

William looked at the form and gulped, "Why do you come to me?"

"Your world is going to be visited by my opposite. His name is Negativity, and he is my ancient brother." the cloud form explained

"But, why have you chosen me for this important job?" William was very confused.

"You have been chosen to fulfill my wishes. That is all you need to know." said the cloud.

"I am but a human. How can I fulfill your wishes?" asked William, wondering if he should pinch himself again, just in case. Surely this thing was mistaken and had come to the wrong person. He couldn't even hit a tree with a rock, let alone fight this Negativity thing.

"My brother has been devouring many souls of humanity and using them to feed his negative power. He is aided by a demon worse then any known to eternity." spoke the cloud.

"The demon's name is King Addictions, and he has been stealing souls and locking them in his dungeons until my brother is ready to devour them!" continued the cloud.

William swallowed hard and asked the cloud again, "How can I, a poor village boy, be of any service to you?"

"I have chosen you to do battle against my ancient brother. You must save humanity from total destruction," answered the cloud.

"How shall I be able to full fill an enormous task such as that?" cried William, feeling a little queasy now.

The cloud replied, "You will not be alone. You will be accompanied by my Positive Beings, which are numerous."

"Many of these Beings you have met before throughout your young life. The very people you are going to help soon introduced you to the Positives. They are Truth, Compassion, Peace, and Love," continued the cloud.

"They come in many forms, but, whatever form they possess, the result is always good and of a positive nature," finished the cloud.

William felt overwhelmed with the task that had just been given to him. He knew in his heart that he could not deny this request. This experience he was having with Positivity was, indeed, real after all, for were there not positive and negative forces in humanity? Both forces were awesome, and, if they were strong enough to provoke the emotions in humans that William experienced every day, then, certainly, they were powerful enough to talk to a human, were they not? Besides, the cloud had said his beloved village was in trouble. Hence, William felt he had no choice. He decided to accept this dangerous task.

Unbeknownst to William, as he was talking with Positivity, the Dark Knight, Sir Denial, was already penetrating his village. The Dark Knight's first goal was to cause the people to lose their respect, by first accepting and then, becoming addicted to the lethal weapons - Alcohol and Drugs. As these weapons attacked the wills and souls of these people, they would see things only through negative eyes, thus, falling under the rule of King Addictions. Once under this spell, they would begin to act as if they had not a care in the world. Hence, Sir Denial was doing his job very well indeed.

Several days after Sir Denial had entered the Village of Honesty and started his horrible task, Sir Death slipped through the gates on a daily basis (by this time, Barthold had succumbed to King Addictions forces and did not care who entered his village).Death's job was to slowly walk through the village and claim whoever's life grew weak from Denial's work. He didn't claim their physical life, for, by the time King Addictions and his Dark Knights got finished with a poor human, the body was but a shell that continued to exist with no hope, happiness or light.

Some souls were stronger than others and could hold on longer, but some, like Henry Tucksworth, were not so strong. Henry's was the first door the horrible Knight knocked on in the Village of Honesty. Henry was the Village shoemaker. When Sir Denial first confronted Henry, he was a quiet, loving man. He lived simply with his wife and two small children. Why he gave in to Sir Denial's weapons, no one truly knows. Some give in because they feel there is something they are missing in the world, and they grow depressed and not so happy with their lives. Others give in because they feel worthless and these weapons make them feel as if they can conquer anything. And yet, still others accept them, because it is what their peers are doing, and they don't want to be the only one not doing it. They want to conform and be accepted.

Whatever the reason, Denial takes advantage of it, as he did with poor Henry the shoemaker, who now was about to meet his fate.

"Who is it that knocks at my door?" asked Henry as he stumbled over all of the shoes that he had neglected to finish while using the weapon Alcohol. You see, my sleeping friend, Death had stopped at Henry's door, because it could sense the doom of an addicted person. Like a hungry wolf sniffing and following the scent of its next pitiful victim, Death was ready to pounce and devour the very thing that separated humanity from the lowly animals, the soul.

Death stood silently at Henry's door for a moment a dark sneer covering its sickly green skull-of-a-face that was hidden beneath its long black robe. Finally it replied, "It is Death, and I have come for the soul of Henry Tucksworth!"

Henry's eyes became wide in fright. He was terrified as he cried,

"This can not be, for I am the village shoemaker!" Henry had denied his fate for a long time. He, like so many others before him, sadly thought that this could never happen to him. This kind of hideous thing only happened to really bad people, and Henry always thought of himself as a good, kind person. The sad truth was - Henry was all of that and more. But the weapons - Alcohol and Drugs - do not discriminate, and, once a person becomes addicted to these weapons, it slowly creeps through to the body and, eventually, captures the heart and muddles the mind until the person loses control of the most important gift they have ever been given - their very being. Once it takes the body, then, it is only a matter of time before the soul is taken.

Henry had now joined the thousands of people who had lost their souls and realized too late that they could have stopped it.

Sir Denial had done his job well!

Henry begged Death to spare his life. "I am not ready to die. I have a wife and children who need me!"

"It is too late for regrets now, human," sneered Death with no pity at all in its voice.

"I will change I will put away Alcohol!" Henry whimpered pathetically.

"You knew Truth, but you chose to follow Denial and accept his weapons, and now it is time to pay with your soul!" There was nothing but glee in the horrible creature's voice.

Death laid its hands on Henry's door and it rotted. The Dark Knight was laughing now, as Henry's wife and children stood by in horror and witnessed the creature in the black robe take the soul from Henry's withering form, and he announced," I want not his body, only his soul, which now belongs to King Addictions. "When my brother arrives there will be no soul to save!" exclaimed Death in an evil voice.

The Dark Knight, Death, spat as he mentioned his brother. You see his brother was also called Death.Natural Death was the true natural Being sent by Positivity. When a human is old and their job is finished in this world or they are sick and seeking release, then Positivity sends Death, and the body and soul are taken at the same time.But when the Dark Knight, Death, is sent by Negativity through King Addictions, the body is left behind as an empty shell.The person's soul is gone to a nightmare of a world, to suffer forever.

After Henry's soul was taken, his family wept in grief.

Once upon a time Henry's wife had a face full of life and radiance. She and their children lived a contented life filled with love and joy until Henry started to loose himself to Alcohol. His once lovely wife and two wonderful children, now only knew desolation and sorrow. To them, Henry was dead long ago, when Addictions crept into his soul. He had become a hollow shell. She had begged and begged Henry to listen to Truth before it was too late, but he had refused to listen.Now she was doomed to live a life without her husband and their little children would grow up without their beloved daddy. So, not only did Denial take a life for King Addictions, he also left a family to suffer the burden. King Addictions was very pleased, indeed, with Denial's work.

CHAPTER THREE

WILLIAM MEETS TRUTH

A few days after his meeting with Positivity, William was strolling through the Village of Honesty contemplating his situation, and he was scared. Had he been dreaming? He looked down at his bruised skin where he had pinched himself. No. He was certain he hadn't been dreaming. After all, did not Henry the shoemaker just die from all those negative things? Didn't Henry's family have to move to the poor house because of the tremendous burden left to them? This thought stirred a feeling in William he didn't quite understand. The way poor Henry died had hurt William. It also made him very angry.

The more he thought about it, the madder he became. As William's anger grew, so did his desire to fight the evil forces that claimed Henry's life. So intent were his thoughts, that you can imagine how startled he was when he happened upon a man...no, not a man, not quite...but, rather, the form of a man surrounded by a great bright white light. This form was sitting on the stone fountain in the Village Square.

"Who are you?" William was half afraid to ask, but ask he did!

"I am Truth, and I was once the foundation of the people of this village," replied the being in a very sad way.

"But you still are the foundation," William insisted.

"Not so," said Truth

"But, you are the foundation of all life," William exclaimed.

"Many of the people in this village do not choose to see me nor do they choose to follow my ways any longer," said Truth

The bright light dimmed as Truth continued, "These people have chosen Sir Denial as their new leader, and all who follow him will surely come to destruction."

As William moved closer to Truth, he could feel the honesty radiating from the Being.In the presence of Truth, William felt free of worry, and, suddenly, he had a vision. The Ocean of Serenity, which bordered the east side of the Village of Honesty, appeared in front of him, and he could feel the peace and endless power of the deep blue waters. William's feeling of contentment changed quickly however, when his vision changed, and he was now beyond the Ocean of Serenity and was facing the Sea of Confusion.

This didn't make sense to William, because he had never seen either of these great bodies of water.He had only learned about them in school, but there they were, as big as life. And, as he attempted to erase the bad vision he was having, Truth took the form of an eagle and said to William, "I must fly throughout the land to learn how much damage has been done by King Addictions and his Knights." Truth bid William good-bye for now, and took flight.

Truth also can take many forms, but, whichever form it takes, it can instill in human kind only good feelings that produced positive results. Truth can be distorted and cruelly used by humans, but, in the end, when the smoke clears, Truth will always come shining through.

William watched as Truth flew off in the distance and decided everything he had seen was real, and he knew that the time had come to begin his travels to the Dark Side of the land to confront King Addictions.Many souls from the land where William was born were imprisoned in the damp and dark dungeons of the Dark King.

The fear and confusion he had been feeling the past few days suddenly turned to determination. The very village who had helped him in his time of need, the very people who had taken him in, and not only fed and clothed him but gave him hugs and kisses when he was hurt and healing herbs when he was sick, these very people needed him now, and he knew he could not turn his back on them. He held is head up and went to pack his few meager belongings, for William fully intended to do battle with Addictions and free as many souls as possible.

THE FALL OF KING NOBODY

One day, when King Nobody was taking one of his daily walks in the country he was approached by a very wise-looking man who was dressed in a white robe. This wise looking man also appeared as if he had lived a good many a years. His snow-white hair came down to his waist, and his silky white beard came down in a growth that touched the earth. Little did the King know, however, that this man's looks were, but, an illusion. The being beneath this illusion was not one of King Addictions' normal Knights. It was, however, very effective and was spending much time in the Land of Nowhere. His name was Deceit.

Now, Deceit was well aware of King Nobody's problems of not knowing his own feelings. It was Deceit who begged King Addictions to give him the job of stealing King Nobody's soul. The great dark King Addictions granted Deceit his request and told him that, if he failed, he would be cast into a hell so hideous that even a demon such as him, would beg for mercy! Deceit agreed.He had a plan to trick King Nobody into thinking he was actually Truth not Deceit.

"Greetings, oh, great one!" said Deceit to King Nobody.

"Greetings, old man, and who might you be?" replied the King.

"I am Truth, and I have felt your troubles with your feelings and have come to help," said Deceit.

"How can you help me when nobody else has been able to?" inquired the King sadly.

"I have a magic potion, and if you swallow it you will gain full knowledge and control of your feelings," said Deceit.

King Nobody suddenly became very interested in what the old man was saying.

"Certainly the price for this potion must be very high," said the king.

"On the contrary," Deceit sneered, "It is but a small price to pay for one's own feelings!"

"So, just what is the price of this potion old man?" King Nobody inquired.

Deceit smiled and answered, "The price is your soul,"

The King was shocked! "That is too high a price to pay!" he shouted.

"I think not, Your Greatness.Without knowing your own feelings, you may never know happiness in this life time!" Deceit answered in a sly way.

Then Deceit added, "The potion will help you find more happiness than you ever even dreamed of!"

Poor desperate King Nobody was weakening. Deceit, sensing the King's weakness, quickly said, "Why be concerned about your soul at present when you can own your own feelings now?"

He held the potion in front of the King and offered it to him. Deep inside, the King had doubts, but he was so tired of feeling nothing that he took the potion that was offered to him to find his feelings. The sad part is that the King had never really lost his feelings. They were in him all the time. He had just never taken the time to notice them.

Deceit triumphantly watched as the King drank the potion that was, in reality, the weapon Alcohol. He knew, that, indeed, the drink would make King Nobody have good feelings temporarily, but his satisfaction was in knowing, that after several good swigs of the so called potion, the good King would be on his way to being enslaved to King Addictions. Once in the grips of Addictions, the King would feel only despair.

Well, after partaking in the potion for quite awhile, the King was hooked!It didn't take long before the effects began to wither his mind and body. Before long the King was bedridden. The King's loyal subjects tried to bring the King back to health, but no matter how hard they searched for a cure, they failed.

"So, you see, young one, the lesson to be learned here is things are not always what they appear. What you may think is true can often be deceit," Said Aggie back at the hospital room.

CHAPTER FOUR

WILLIAM'S JOURNEY BEGINS

William waited until daybreak before he began his long journey to the Village of Negativity in the Dark Land, where he would confront King Addictions. The Dark Village existed along the coast of the Sea of Confusion, and, unfortunately, William would have to cross this dreadful sea before he could enter the Dark Land where King Addictions lived. The only comfort was that he would first be sailing the Ocean of Serenity. This pure body of deep, crystal blue water was always peaceful and serene. William was looking forward to that leg of his long journey, for he would never forget the day, long ago, when he was but a wee lad that his parents had taken a holiday and sailed the Ocean of Serenity. Though he was very young he will never forget the peace and contentment they emitted when they returned and, oh, the wonderful stories they had told him. His heart was joyful as he thought back to that day, but it suddenly grew heavy as he also remembered it was not long after that, that he had lost them.

William squinted against the sun, placing his hand above his brow to block the bright light and allow him to see what was ahead. It was then that he realized the sun had set, and he smiled because that meant he had finally reached his first destination, the Village of Hope. It was from here that he would set sail for the Dark Land in the morning, but, until then, he was overjoyed at the thought of visiting with his old friend who lived there and had visited him many times during his darkest hours. Her name was Compassion.

William had never been to the Village of Hope before. Alas, he had never been anywhere outside his village, but he had heard about the village called Hope. It was supposed to be very scenic and, inside its beautiful white stonewalls, a light forever shined on this village. For, within the walls of the village, there was nothing but good tidings and Positive Beings. It was this light that blinded him now, and William hurried on, anxious to get there, for he had traveled all day on foot and was weary and in need of food. William smiled as he thought about Compassion. He envisioned her eyes that were as deep blue as the Ocean of Serenity. Her face shone with age and the long blue velvet robe that she wore was tattered from all the battles she had fought against her fiercest enemy Ignorance. Compassion had comforted many a human Being during their time of need and suffering. When the Creator formed her and first sent her out into the word, her job had been to help those who had suffered a terrible loss and who's pain had left a big hole in there soul. But, ever since the darkness started to invade the lands, her job had expanded to fight Ignorance, who gleefully afflicted humankind and caused the people to make horrible judgments against each other before they knew all of the facts. People who were victims of Ignorance were hurt physically and emotionally, and it was then that Compassion would appear to ease their pain and give them comfort.

William knew that Compassion could not always seen by the human eye, but her work was always showing itself in positive ways. Sometimes at night, when the stars were out and there was an evening breeze, you could hear Compassion's voice on the wind as she was saying, "Oh, Ignorance, you foul and evil creature, how many tears you have brought to humankind!"

Lately, Ignorance had grown much fiercer, causing wars, death and destruction to humankind that had frightened William. But Compassion had eased his fears saying, "Dear William, it is certain that humankind will never be rid of Ignorance, but I promise you that I will always be here to ease the pain and sorrow brought on by this Dark Being."

As if his thoughts had summoned her, Compassion met William at the Golden Gate that sat at the entrance of the Village of Hope.

"Greetings!" cried William with a sincere grin.

"Welcome, William" replied Compassion.

"It has been a long and hard journey from my village, and the news I have is very sad,"

"I have heard the voice of Positivity on the wind and know of your quest," said Compassion.

"I am afraid to face Addictions," said William in a shaky voice.

"I hope that your village will not remain in its present state, and that, with the help of other Positive Beings, you will be able to face and defeat King Addictions," replied Compassion.

Once again, William told Compassion that he was afraid, but, after seeing his village cast into ruins, he was also very angry and willing to go up against Addictions with everything he had.

"My work has been very difficult and never ceasing these days, more so than in past times. Addictions had cast a shadow over the land, and there are many who have need of my help!" said Compassion.

"I have heard it said that in this village, the Village of Hope, that King Addictions' power is weak. Is this true?" inquired William.

"It is true, child, for the very sight of Hope overwhelms King Addictions with Fear. In this village, Addictions' own Dark Knight will turn against him!" replied Compassion.

"I must sail the Ocean of Serenity and the Sea of Confusion to reach my inevitable destiny on the Dark Side of the land to the Dark Land of King Addictions." said William.

William thanked Compassion for her comfort and started off to the town's center on foot. While walking on the cobble stone streets towards the center of town, William chanced to see other Positive Beings that were in the village at the time.

The being, Peace, was in the Village of Hope talking with Happiness. At this time, Peace had taken the form of a human, but this human was a giant. The arms of the giant were huge and strong. The being had on a silver robe. His face was pure and his eyes a determined hazel which complimented his thick black head of hair that was lying wildly on his head. On the back of the Being, Peace, there appeared a world of which apparently Peace was the keeper. As Peace spoke in a loud thunderous voice which reached to the heavens, he proclaimed,

"Many battles and much death and violence have I seen through all of time, but never will I cease to carry the world of the humans for, surely, in the end, Peace will be the foundation of all life!"

Happiness, still in its own form, was not to be seen by the human eye, but, where this Being dwelt, the space of air that it existed in was sweet and nourishing, and the land upon which Happiness stood became immediately fresher, the grass greener and the flowers more colorful. Everywhere, at any time Happiness was around, things became better, stronger and more productive, including, I might add, human beings. Certainly life can be grand if we would change our perception of it from our souls. For what radiates from our soul, affects our entire being and what affects our whole being affects other beings. Happiness can rapidly spread to other souls and cause wide spread Happiness. Impossible you say? If Sadness can spread, so can Happiness!

Love in its spirit form was also in the village. Love appeared as a bright white light whispering through the air and carrying with it feelings of unconditional love and acceptance.

"I offer Love to all existence, but Hate makes itself easier to use, henceforth, some in humanity choose to hate. Hate eats at the very core of humanity while it drains the very life force from people without solving any problems," whispered Love.

Love continued,

"If any human being chooses me over Hate, a prosperous and long life they will have!"

After Love finished talking, Happiness began to take on human form. In this human form, Happiness appeared as a human female in the third year of age with brown silky hair and bright green eyes. The child appeared most innocent and happy - truly a child seeing life in all its wonders. Happiness, as a small child, began to speak. "I came as a child. Hate has not yet been able to present itself to me as it has to adults," said Happiness. "One thing I know, humanity does not learn how to love. They are born with the ability, but they do learn how to hate!" continued Happiness.

N finishing, Happiness said,

"Henceforth, as a child in the eyes of humanity, I shall remain to let humanity know that every time they cast their eyes on a child, hate can be unlearned as well as learned!"

After listening to these Positive Beings and listening to them speak, William felt his task would truly be lighter with this knowledge. William left and went to the Village Inn for rest and nourishment after his long journey to the Village of Hope.

At the same time William was getting a much needed rest, in another village in the Land of Nowhere, the continuing problem of Addictions was making itself known. The village, to be precise, was the Village of Security.

"Who are you?" asked Stephen, the stable man, in a sarcastic tone.

"You do not drink the magic potion or use the other magic potions given to us by our friend the farmer!" continued Stephen.

"I am Danielle, and I do not want to use the magic potions. For, after seeing what price my fellow villagers are paying, the magic is not worth the price!"

"Then, why do you stay among us?" asked Nathaniel (also from the village). "You are not like us, and your unwilling presence amongst us bothers us greatly," returned Stephen.

As tears were forming in her eyes, Danielle replied,

"Our Village of Security is quickly becoming a village of false security. Once our streams ran clean and pure down the side of the hill and the town's people farmed the land at the bottom of the hill and tended to the forest and every day was a beautiful and productive day, Nathaniel!"

"You and Stephen have changed. So have many people in the village and the magic potion is first on the minds of many!" continued Danielle.

Close by and hiding in the woods, the Dark Knight, Sir Denial, was laughing and thinking, "These people will never see the truth. My power is too strong!"

"The farmer who gave us this potion said that there would be small prices to pay, but it is worth it for the good feelings his magic gives us!" said Stephen.

"Danielle, who was very obviously upset, was fifteen years of age. Her parents were still alive but under the influence of King Addictions. Danielle's long black hair was laid wildly on her head, and her steel green eyes were set in a serious manner as she replied, "You are giving away your souls. The farmer deceives you!"

At this, the two village men became furious.

"If you will not join us, then take your leave of this village, and do not cry to your Mother or Father, for they use the potion and are on our side!" Nathaniel shouted in an angry voice.

"Your Mother and Father use the magic and still you do not see the true way!" exclaimed Stephen.

"So. Be banished from this village forever, and feel the harsh hand of rejection!" shouted Nathaniel as he was pushing Danielle towards the gates of the village.

And, so it was that Danielle was shunned by the entire village and cast out the Village Of Serenity. Danielle decided to take her leave that very morning and travel to the only place she felt that she would be comforted which was the Village of Hope.

CHAPTER FIVE

KING ADDICTIONS REJOICES

"Souls, souls, and more souls, and still they keep coming," said Addictions jubilantly. Now, on this dark and dreary night at the castle on the Dark Side of the land, King Addictions was celebrating the multitude of souls he was winning over to himself. On this night the evil King joined with all of his negative Knights, and they became as one. It has been said that when King Addictions is in this state of being, any human upon sight of the King would die of fright.

"Come all of my Knights and for this short period let us be as one to reaffirm our purpose on this earth of mortals!" After joining with his Knights, King Addictions released them one by one until; once again, they were separate beings.

"I am well pleased with your accomplishments!" King Addictions said to his Knights

"Listen to the souls crying for mercy. They are in a living nightmare of which there is no escape!" exclaimed Fear, above the laughter of the other Dark Knights.

"Yes. And with the Ancient Master, Negativity, behind us, we will lay this pathetic world to waste!" exclaimed the demon, Alcohol.

"Do not forget me my Brother, I also have lain to waste to many a soul." cackled the demon, Drugs. The King and his Knights celebrated by gathering some of the souls that Death had delivered and taking them to the deepest pit in the castle - to the dungeons. Addictions and his Knights took the souls to what humans know to be hell. At the entrance to the dungeons was a gatekeeper. The gatekeeper was named Insanity.

Insanity appeared as a body with a multitude of faces setting on top of many necks. All of the faces were hideous looking and biting at each other's face. The faces were all saying different things,

"Welcome to eternal damnation!" one face said.

"We will serve you agony which no human is capable of imagining," another face would say.

"Come in and play with us!" yet another face would say.

The poor souls were screaming in agony when King Addictions shouted, "Open the gate Insanity or face the pain of Negativity!" This thing called Insanity grabbed a key chain from around its waste and picked out the key to the dungeons. The thing then wobbled over to the dungeon door and opened it. Insanity wobbled because it had no legs. It had only arms, and they were huge and strong to prevent any of the souls from escaping.

After the souls spent time in the dungeons suffering they would be turned over to Negativity. Outside of the dungeons and in a deeper level of the castle than the dungeons, a huge bottomless pit existed.It was at this pit that Addictions spoke to the Ancient Master, Negativity. As the King and his Dark Knights formed a circle around this pit, mud, dust, and a very sickly smell arose from the pit.

"Oh, most exalted ruler of the Dark Universe, I, Addictions, has come to make an offering of human souls!" shouted Addictions in glee.

Suddenly, the whole of Nowhere land became very dark and the clouds in the sky began moving at a quick pace, and, as the presence of Negativity made known itself, Fear was released to run at will amongst the land, and there came from the land crying and screaming of the people being struck by Fear. A hideous voice belched itself up from the bowels of the pit in the Dark Castle and spoke in a thunderous way,"In the beginning, there was only Darkness. Then a freakish accident happened, and there was Light, but Darkness is stronger than Light and, in the end, there will be only Darkness!"

Addictions and his Knights fell down on their knees, for now, even their Dark Friend, Fear, turned on them!

"Cast in more souls and make haste Addictions. I, Negativity, hunger for food to increase my power over the Universe." said Negativity in an evil and thunderous voice.

At this time, some of the souls were cast into the pit and some were left in the dungeons.

As the souls were cast into the pit they screamed in terror, but the only response from Addictions was laughter.

"Souls and more souls, oh, how easy it is to steal them, while these pathetic humans put everything first before trying to stop me!" shouted Addictions in a hideous way.

"Silence!" you fool. Even as we speak, my brother plots against me!" warned Negativity.

"Worry not, my Ancient Master. The gathering of souls goes well!" said Addictions.

"I know of the work you do Addictions, and that is in your favor, but you would do well not to boast yet!" warned Negativity.

"The purpose of my existence is to please you my Ancient Master!" said Addictions, in a voice that sounded victorious.

"Hear me well, Addictions. You are my most powerful weapon against Positivity, but there is much work to do before the battle is won," said Negativity.

"This is true Ancient Master. Your brother will use all of his positive Knights against you!" exclaimed Addictions.

"Happiness, Truth, Love and the rest of his Knights cause me to vomit goodness!" said Negativity in a mocking voice.

"They will bow before us in the end, oh, Ancient Master!" replied Addictions, in a sarcastic voice.

"Go now, King Addictions, and spread throughout the land the only real truth in life which is, that life is, and always will be, miserable!" finished Negativity in a thunderous voice.

"Oh. Yes, my Ancient Master. I will continue to destroy until all is forever lost!" answered Addictions.

With these parting words, the Dark King proceeded to disperse his Knights and continue his work. As Negativity began to descend into the pit, its voice followed loudly at first and then fading as it descended the pit,

"Destroy... destroy...destroy."

CHAPTER SIX

DANIELLE MEETS DENIAL

In the meantime, Danielle, having been banished from her village, was traveling along the road that would take her to the Village of Hope. Along the way she happened to meet a farmer. The farmer appeared meek and harmless.

"Greetings, my good lady," said the farmer in a shy way.

"Greeting," replied Danielle in a friendly voice.

"I am a meek and poor farmer looking to sell my goods in the next village I come to," said the farmer.

At the time of this meeting, the night was just beginning to cover the world with a dark blanket and the sun was slowly falling behind the mountains." I am Danielle from the Village of Security, and I am traveling to the Village of Hope to seek hope to go on in Life!" said Danielle with tears in her eyes.

"What troubles you my child?" asked the farmer.

"I am hurt because my peers have rejected me and cast me out from my home!" replied Danielle, still very upset.

"Weep not, my young friend, for I have the answer to your problem", said the farmer.

"You do?" inquired Danielle.

"Yes, my child. You see, I know the pain you suffer and the fear and sadness you feel!" said the farmer.

"Were you cast out from your home too?" asked Danielle.

At this time, the farmer went into an act. He began looking very sad and in despair as he looked at Danielle with sad eyes and said, "People can be so cruel and uncaring, and they do not easily give love, and the pain of this reality is almost unbearable!"

After his speech the farmer began to smile to himself in an evil way. The evil could not be seen for it was inside the farmers very being. The farmer then looked at Danielle and said,

"I, being a wise and loving person, will offer you my magic potions, and you will not have to feel reality ever again." said the farmer, with a false compassionate look about him.

"What kind of potions?" Danielle asked.

"Why, my friend's of course," the farmer said shrewdly. The farmer knew he had Danielle's attention.

"My friends care not how you look or who you are.Nor do they make unreasonable demands on you!" said the farmer.

"Who are your friends?" asked Danielle.

"See now for yourself. Come out and make known your presence my friends!" the farmer shouted. At this time two farm boys came out of a nearby forest and stood in front of Danielle.

"This, my dear child, is Alcohol and his Brother, Drugs. Alcohol will give you a feeling of warmth and will make all of your problems vanish", said the farmerDanielle was beginning to feel uneasy at this point.

"On the other hand, Drugs can make you feel, up, down, slow, fast, somewhat out of reality or all the way out of reality!" Beginning to get excited, the farmer's voice became louder.

"You can have pot, cocaine, acid, horse, uppers, downers, speed or anything your heart desires," spoke the farmer.

At this point the farmer started dancing around in a frantic way and said,"Pot will make you laugh. Cocaine will give you endless energy."By accident, the farmer let his words slip and said, "And, when you are in chains, you will not be able to stop using any of these Drugs!"

"Stop! I know of your friends. They are destroying my village and killing my loved ones," cried Danielle.

The farmer stopped dancing and began to get an angry look upon his face.

"Your price for using the magic potions is death, insanity and ruined families. You offer people a false and temporary escape from reality and then steal their souls from their very body!" shouted Danielle.

CHAPTER SEVEN

DENIAL SHOWS HIS FACE

At this time, the farmer's appearance began to change. The farmer's body became very thin and lanky. His face was the color of putrid green. His eyes were mirrors reflecting the ruined lives of his past victims. A hideous grin appeared on the Dark Being's face. And, although the being was six foot tall, its shoulders were hunched and its arms were long. The Dark Knight's arms ended with long green hands that had long uncut and dirty fingernails. The farmer thing then opened its mouth to the Heavens and shouted all means of abominable words toward the sky. The farmer was in reality the Dark Knight called Denial.

After cursing all that was good, Denial focused its attention on Danielle and began to speak. "Foolish little girl. I offer you an escape from this miserable, stinking life of yours, and you refuse!" As Denial spoke, the very trees, around the evil being, rotted and died. Denial, once again, began to shout foul words, and, as it did, its teeth rattled loudly. Danielle was now very frightened but gathered enough courage to speak her mind to this vile being.

"The escape you offer is temporary and demands life itself in return. The people you deceive have no control over their own lives. They see things that are not really there. They do things they cannot even remember doing. And then, from the inside to the outside, they rot away to nothing and leave the soul to King Addictions

Denial began to laugh hideously. Then he spoke, "I do love to watch them when they are trembling from head to toe and are in emotional torment, especially when they give up the fight and come back to us for more." Denial stopped as if to think about things, and then continued,

"When they try to get help, other people tell them they are either morally weak or spiritually weak and all they need to do is not use our potions anymore and that advice is the very thing that fills them full of hurt and sends them back to us." Denial was so giddy over his own words he was beside himself. "Stupid, arrogant, pathetic human beings think they can help their own kind by telling them to just quit using the potions." Denial concluded. As the Dark Knight was laughing, a light began to form in a nearby forest. The light took the form of a cloud and began drifting towards them. The cloud stopped in front of Denial causing the Dark Knight much fear.

The cloud spoke,

"Leave this child and return to the pit of hell where you belong!"

Upon seeing and hearing the cloud, Denial screamed in agony and spoke, "Take leave of this place, Truth. You have no business here!"

"The cry of an innocent child's soul has called too me and begs me to intercede," replied Truth.

"Let the child help herself!" screamed Denial.

"I will always hear the cry of one who believes in me, and, surely, I will help her," replied Truth, in a soft confident voice.

"This human is mine!" shouted Denial. "Flee from this place before I call on the Ancient Master, Positivity, to destroy you!" warned Truth. Taking on the form of a dark storm cloud, Denial flew with the wind in the direction of the Dark Side of the land to the castle of Addictions to report what had happened.

While fleeing Denial shouted to Truth, You have not defeated me. You have only put off what is meant to be, for I am the way to eternal damnation, and there is no other way!"

After Denial and his two companions Alcohol and Drugs - had fled, Danielle thanked Truth for saving her from Denial.

"Continue your journey with haste my child, for, as you have learned here today, the Truth is not always easy to follow," spoke Truth, in a soft voice.

"At first, I did think the farmer was telling the truth!" said Danielle.

"Many attempts are made to deceive me, but, in the end, when the smoke clears, I will be there still. Humans can distort me and hide me for many years, but they cannot change me. Sooner or later it will be me they see!" spoke Truth.

Danielle was exhausted from her encounter with Denial and decided that Truth was certainly not easy to follow. However, she did feel very good about herself now and was glad that she decided to follow the Truth. Danielle also discovered that Truth dwelt within her being all of the time, and she need only call for it when she needed it. Danielle bid goodbye to Truth and made haste on the continuation of her journey. At this same time in the Village of Hope, William was awakening from a much-needed sleep and had no idea that he would meet Danielle in person that very day. Over on the Good Side of the land, a Dark Shadow was continuing to grow. It was now covering most of the Land of Nowhere. However, for a brief period of time during Danielle's encounter with Truth, the sunlight broke through the center of the Darkness and shined radiantly throughout the Land of Nowhere.

CHAPTER EIGHT

NEGATIVITY IS ANGERED

At the same time, in the land that King Addictions ruled, the ground was quaking, and Negative Beings howled in misery. Lightening bolts struck the ground around the castle, and the bodies of the dead at the hands of Addictions rose and walked the earth chanting, "We have died in vain and our souls are forever lost."

As the dead were walking the earth they were also chanting "Behold the power of Positivity, for, surely, he will be dominant in the end!"

Suddenly, in the front of King Addictions' castle, a huge crack in the ground appeared, and, as it was getting larger, a thunderous voice came out of it and spoke,

"I have been stricken with Truth and wounded by goodness!"

The voice coming from the opening in the ground was so thunderous that it leveled trees and mountains. The voice was so hideous and loud that the dead, once again, became silent. It was Negativity's voice coming from the crack in the earth and the whole of the land heard it. The Good and the Bad, the Dead and the Living were all stricken by the Dark Knight, Fear. King Addictions heard the voice and went into hiding. All of existence heard the voice of Negativity.

"Listen too me. None have died in vain. The ones who have died by the hand of

Addictions have become one with me, and together will dominate Eternity!" People who were asleep at the time also heard the voice of Negativity,

"Listen well," said Negativity," There is no good, only bad and happy does not exist. Hope is dead and only despair lives. Truth does no good

It only deceives people into thinking all-is-well, and then, I destroy their hopes!" People throughout the land were trembling with fear and the ones who were asleep were stuck in a nightmare. Negativity then bellowed out a hideous laugh and spoke again.

"You see no Hope. You see in your past only wars, and you see in your present only people murdering other people. You see Hate, Greed and Murder," continued Negativity.

All at once, the skies all over nowhere land became as mirrors. The mirrors reflected all that was negative about nowhere land. On the mirrors were scenes of neglected children, broken homes, mentally ill and other handicapped people being treated like animals. After allowing the people of the land to view these reflected images, Negativity spoke once again,

"All ye people in the Land of Nowhere, look to the sky and remember that there is no Hope. There is only my Truth. Positive Knights do not exist. There is only me." Negativity was mocking all that was good.

"Where are all of the Positive Beings? I see them not. They care not about you!" mocked Negativity.

Not one of the humans challenged the Ancient Master, for they knew that it would mean instant destruction.

"I have shown you only a small amount of my power. My power exists in every fiber of every Universe, and I am foolishly underestimated!" roared Negativity.

It was true. Addictions, for instance, was viewed as a weakness that could be overcome with will power. Once again, the ancient Dark Master began to speak,

"The reason that Addictions is so powerful is because nobody believes in him.No matter how much destruction he brings, humans close their eyes and pretend that Addictions does not exist. They call it Addictions, but they do not believe it!" Once again, the mirrors became active in the sky. This time a scene was being played. The scene began with a conversation between two humans. The first human was speaking to a friend about another friend's Alcohol problem. The first human said, "I think our friend Patrick has a problem with Alcohol." He is just weak-willed and no good. He has no problem only a weak mind. Anyway, it is common knowledge that there is no real disease called Addictions. It is all in his mind!" replied the second human. Even now after all that you have heard, many will not believe in Addictions, and, surely, I will command Addictions to continue destroying until no soul remains untouched!" spoke Negativity.

"You cannot defeat something that you do not believe in, and, surely, my Dark Knight, Denial, will see that you never believe in Addictions." finished Negativity. At this time, the mirrors in the sky vanished and the voice of the ancient Dark Master trailed off as it descended back into the pit. As Negativity descended the pit it was chanting,

"Destroy...destroy...destroy."

The ground once again became as it was before Negativity arose from it. Afterwards, many people of the Land of Nowhere decided that they had been dreaming and that the whole experience was just a nightmare from which they had awakened.But souls captured by Addictions could never wake up. They lived in an eternal nightmare.

CHAPTER NINE

A MEETING OF THE POSITIVE BEINGS

Shortly after seeing the display of the awesome power of Negativity, Peace and Love were talking to each other in the Village of Hope, and they both saw how serious the situation was becoming.

"We must tell Hope what has taken place, and we need to do it fast!" exclaimed Peace.

"Yes. Negativity's power grows strong, and he is trying to swallow up the entire Universe for his evil purpose of growing stronger," replied Love.

"If we do not act soon, Negativity will turn all known worlds into a living nightmare!" exclaimed Peace. "Even beyond the Land of Nowhere."

"If he accomplishes that, nowhere land will be "Nowhere" for the end of time!" replied Love.

"There is no need to seek me out my friends, for I have felt the power of Negativity, and I must take flight to the four corners of the world and call all positive beings to help in our fight against the ancient Dark Master!" said Hope who was there unseen, listening to the conversation. Hope then took on the form of a unicorn with a strong muscular body of pure white. The wings of the unicorn had a ten-foot span and its eyes were a deep blue.

If the eyes of the unicorn were looked into, they would appear as endless as an ocean.

"My eyes see only goodness, and the goodness they see, will never end!" said Hope.

The stage was set and a fierce battle was beginning to take shape. A battle although unseen, takes place in our towns and cities every day. A battle that we cannot see but we can certainly see the results of the battle - people dying, families broken apart, jails and prisons filling up and innocent victims getting caught up in the battle every day. It is the battle with Addictions.

CHAPTER TEN

THE SEA OF CONFUSION

After a long and dangerous journey, Danielle finally arrived at the Village of Hope. Danielle was very tired and hungry, so she stopped at the first inn that she found in the Village of Hope. Upon finding the inn, she entered through the front door and found a table to sit down at. At the same time William was also eating at the same inn. William was building his strength for what lay ahead for him. William was also gathering courage for the journey by ship across the Sea of Confusion.

While eating, William chanced to see Danielle eating at another table. He felt that she was troubled about something so he spoke to her,

"You look like a weary soul!" he said.

Danielle looked at William. She thought to herself, "He looks honest enough. Maybe he can help me save my village."

"I am very weary sir, and who might you be?" asked Danielle.

"I am William, and I am from the Village of Honesty,

"At least you have a Village. I have been put out of my home!" said Danielle.

"Why have you been cast out?" inquired William.

"I have been cast out for not taking the magic potions that the rest of the village is taking." said Danielle.

"I see that your village is also under attack by King Addictions and his Dark Knights!" said William.

"Have you also been cast out?" asked Danielle.

"No. I have been sent away from my village to cross the Sea of Confusion and to do battle with Addictions," replied William.

Upon hearing what William had said, Danielle felt an inner peace because now she knew that there was a name for the problem her village was having, and it was Addictions.

"Please sir, I must join you in your quest, for everything and everyone I love has been brought to ruins by King Addictions." pleaded Danielle.

"The journey is a dangerous one, and we may be destroyed!" warned William.

William looked at Danielle and saw Hope in her eyes.

"Truly this is an honest person," he thought to himself.

"Very well. You are welcome to join in this quest!" said William.

The rest of that evening Danielle and William spent getting to know each other and planning for the next day when they would set sail for the sea of Confusion. Danielle was finally able to eat and get some rest after spending some time with William, her new- found friend. Danielle knew that now she was not in this alone!

The following day in the Village of Hope, as the sun came up; the sky and the entire landscape were very colorful. Down by the dock, where the ship, called the Vessel of Truth was docked and waiting for its passengers - all of the townspeople were gathered. Each and every one of the townspeople knew at least one or more persons who were destroyed by Addictions and were more than eager to watch William and Danielle start their journey. The townspeople told William and Danielle that they would be willing to help in any way they could.

The Vessel of Truth was a huge ship that was made of solid wood. The ship had large white sails and was put together well. The Vessel of Truth required no one to sail it, for the spirit of Truth did the navigating.

As William and Danielle came down to greet the people, the entire village was cheering for them. After spending some time with the people of the village, William and Danielle headed for the ship. As the plank of the ship lowered, all the people of the village cheered for the two brave souls who were embarking on this dangerous journey. William turned and faced the people of the village and shouted,

"Better to die fighting King Addictions than to become his victim!" When the two brave souls were on board, the ship set sail with nobody at the helm. The destination was the Sea of Confusion, and the captain of the ship was Truth. The ship first had to sail over the Ocean of Serenity in order to get to the Sea of Confusion.

The Ocean of Serenity was a very peaceful place. The souls who lived in the ocean were always at peace and were happy. William and Danielle would sit out on the ship's deck at night and look at the stars. During the daytime the sea was always calm with a mild wind to move the ship along. The skies were always a deep blue and the ocean was always very awake with many inhabitants. The souls in the Ocean of Serenity were always happy, because they did not believe in opinions. They thought opinions were varied and confusing. Whenever a problem came up in the ocean, the souls would get together and decide on one solution that made everybody happy. Thus the ocean always remained serene.

The journey on the Ocean of Serenity went without incident. The ocean remained calm and the skies remained blue. One day, William was standing up at the front of the ship watching the ocean, and a voice whispered to him,

"William, prepare you for the Keeper of the Strait of Choice."

"Who is the Keeper?" asked William.

"The Keeper is a Negative Being, and he will seek to destroy you. He will give you a choice first, but then he will try to destroy you!" said Truth.

"What should we do to avoid destruction?" inquired William.

"The only way to avoid destruction is to be silent and listen to my voice," said Truth.

Danielle, who was below the deck of the ship, also heard the voice of Truth. Danielle went up on deck and joined William. She walked up to William and held his hand and looked at him and said, "I am ready for the Keeper of the Strait of Choice."

"That is good, for soon we will meet him!" exclaimed William.

CHAPTER ELEVEN

WILLIAM AND DANIELLE MEET THE KEEPER OF THE STRAIT

After three days of peaceful sailing while William and Danielle were below the deck in the area of the ship where they cooked their food, they noticed that the ship was tossing on the waves more than usual. Upon going up on deck, they noticed that the skies had turned dark and stormy. The waves in the ocean were getting choppy and rough. Soon the ship was getting tossed around on the ocean like a toy. The wind was getting very strong and to avoid getting blown off the ship and into the ocean, William and Danielle went below deck. Below the deck the two brave souls awaited the voice of Truth. While waiting for the voice of Truth, the ship just suddenly stopped moving, and it was as if it was being held in one spot on the ocean. Soon after the ship stopped a thunderous voice roared from the dark sky,

"Who is it that sails on the Vessel of Truth?" the voice roared. William and Danielle remained silent, waiting for Truth.

"Who is it that dares face me?" the Keeper roared.

Below the deck of the ship, William and Danielle heard the voice of Truth,

"Go up on the deck and make yourselves seen or you will be destroyed without a second thought from the keeper!" whispered Truth. With some hesitation the two brave souls went up to the deck of the ship to face the Keeper. Upon reaching the deck of the ship, Danielle looked around and saw that all of life, except for her and William, had just stopped! The ship had stopped moving. The ocean was at a standstill. And the sky was as still as an oil painting. William looked up and saw a huge dark cloud in the shape of a human male. Lightening lit up the visions eyes, and the Keeper saw William and Danielle. The dark cloud made if's way closer to the ship and spoke. "Fools. I could crush your pathetic ship and kill both of you!" said the Keeper.

At this time Danielle heard the voice of Truth, and replied to the keeper, "You are bound by nature to allow us one choice before you can do anything further!" Upon hearing this, the Keeper became angry and hurled lightening bolts at the ocean around the ship and roared in anger throughout the dark sky. The roars of the Keeper were thunder, and the ocean became rough again. All of this once again ceased. After a few minutes had passed, William and Danielle thought that their end was near. The Keeper then spoke. "It is true. I am bound to grant you one choice," roared the Keeper. William also heard what Truth had said, so he gathered all the air in his lungs he could gather and shouted to the Keeper,

"We choose to sail the Sea of Confusion!"

The Keeper began laughing loudly, and his laugh was so powerful that it reached the four corners of the world. After awhile the Keeper grew weary, and the laughing stopped. The Keeper then looked toward William and said,

"Your choice is granted, for surely the choice you made will be your destruction!" roared the Keeper.

"Maybe so, but it is our choice to make!" shouted William.

"You could have chosen the Ocean of Serenity, but instead, you have chosen eternal misery!" the Keeper roared.

The Keeper had orders from Negativity to follow the ship into the Sea of Confusion and crush it, casting the souls of William and Danielle into the Sea.

"Enter into the strait. It will take you to the Sea of Confusion," said the Keeper. The Keeper then moved away from the ship and allowed the Vessel of Truth to pass through the gate and into the strait. The Vessel of Truth then sailed into the strait. The journey through the strait was an untroubled journey. During the entire journey the waters were calm and the sky was clear. William and Danielle welcomed the relief; however, they were not aware that the Keeper, who was at this point unable to be seen by the human eye, was following them! At the end of the journey as the ship was nearing the Sea of

Confusion, the water, once again, became rough and choppy and the skies became dark.In the distance, William and Danielle thought that they could hear humans crying in pain and wailing in misery.The closer their ship got, the louder the sounds of the lost souls sounded.

Upon entering the Sea of Confusion, the wailing of the lost souls was very loud. William looked out toward the sea and saw millions of lost souls in agony. Some of the lost souls sensed the Truth on board of the ship and attempted to climb aboard the ship. Whenever one of the lost souls would get close to getting on the ship, a hideous looking creature would knock the soul back into the sea. The skies above the Sea of Confusion were full of these hideous creatures. These creatures were the creation of King Addictions. Opinions were all these creatures had to offer, and none of their opinions solved any problem. They only kept the lost souls confused. Thus, the name given to these creatures was Opinion Creatures.

The Opinion Creatures had heads that had no faces on them. There was skin on their heads, but they had no ears, eyes, or noses. They only had a mouth, and it was large and full of razor sharp teeth. These creatures also had huge wings that resembled the wings of a bat. Their arms were long and lanky, and their hands had long and very sharp fingernails.Their mouths were always shaped in a contorted grin. The foot of an Opinion Creature looked like a human hand a hand that grew off of long muscular legs. William and Danielle could hear them shouting in the sky. They were shouting at each other. You see, they all had different opinions and none of them could agree on any one thing. At night they would swoop out of the sky and attached themselves onto some of the lost souls. Upon attaching to a lost soul, they would laugh while they were tormenting the soul. They slashed into the souls and bit them all night long. The lost souls could not move during these times at night. They could only be still and scream into the night.

The lost souls were in a hell of many different opinions but were never able to decide which opinion was the right one! When one of the lost souls attempted to climb the side of the ship, a group of Opinion Creatures would fly down and start giving opinions. One creature would say,

"If you loved God, you would not belong to Addictions!"

Another Opinion Creature would say, "Just quit using drugs and alcohol."

Yet, another would say, "You are a weak person, and that is all you will ever be!" Upon becoming confused with all of the opinions, the lost souls would fall back into the sea. So it is in our reality. The clergyman tells you to trust God and give up the addiction. The psychiatrist wants to put addicted people on more drugs. The doctor tells a person to just quit using alcohol and drugs. It only takes will power.The only thing these people have in common is their lack of ability to come together for the good of the person suffering. William and Danielle were holding each other for comfort when Truth once again spoke, "William...William... One of the lost souls has seen me. This soul is no longer lost and will be on the deck soon. Go greet him. He could be a powerful ally in your battle against Addictions." spoke Truth

CHAPTER TWELVE

ZOM COMES ABOARD THE SHIP

William and Danielle waited until the being climbed on board the ship. Then they went to greet him.

"Who are you?" asked William.

"I am Zom and belong to the people of the deep." What is a creature of the deep doing in the Sea of Confusion?" asked Danielle.

"My people, too, have been stricken by Addictions. It is a long story, and when we have more time to spare, I shall share it with you. In the meantime, we need to get away from this sea!" said Zom.

"We cannot leave. This sea must be sailed before we get to the Dark Land!" said William

"I have been swimming in this hell for a long time until I saw the light of Truth. It was the light which helped me to escape this sea."

"Why do you want to stay here?" inquired Zom. William explained to Zom that they must cross the sea to reach the Dark Land and do battle with King Addictions and his Dark Knights.

The creature of the deep did not look human. It was at least six feet tall, and his body was green. Zom could breathe in or out of the water with his gills that were on the sides of his chest. Zom had webbed feet and hands and eyes of deep blue. The creatures arms and legs were very strong looking and powerful. Danielle introduced herself and William to the creature. The creature asked them why they were going to the Dark Land. William told the creature that they were going to do battle with Addictions. Zom thought over what he had just heard, and after thinking for a few minutes, he replied, "This King Addictions destroyed my home on land and drove my people to the deepest part of this sea. I shall join this battle!"

Danielle knew that this creature was now their friend.

"I no longer fear Addictions, for now I know Truth!" said Danielle. "Very well, my newfound friend, you can join us in our quest to defeat Addictions and free millions of souls!" exclaimed William.

Upon hearing of the new soul joining with William and Danielle, the Gatekeeper became angry. A thunderous voice came from nowhere and everywhere, and it said,

"I, the Gatekeeper, will now destroy you and your ship!"

Dark clouds came down over the ship and there was a storm in the making, and it was the Gatekeeper! It was the worst storm yet.

Lightening was hurled toward the ship and was making direct hits. The wind picked up to hurricane force, and the waves were higher then the ship. William and his companions ran below deck to seek protection from the storm.

"William…William…. Do not fear Death, for I have death bound in chains at this time. Tell the Opinion Creatures the truth. Tell them that when King Addictions no longer has need for them. He will have the Gatekeeper cast them into the eternal dark pit to live in hell with Negativity!" whispered Truth.

Soon after hearing Truth speak, William hurried above to the deck of the ship and started climbing to the crows nest. Upon reaching the crows-nest, William began shouting in a loud voice.

"Hear me. The Gatekeeper means to destroy all of you. When the Gatekeeper is done with your services, he will destroy all of the Opinion Creatures!" William shouted loud and repeated himself until he was sure the Opinion Creatures had heard it. The Gatekeeper also heard what William was shouting. "Listen to him not. He lies and seeks to confuse you!" shouted the Gatekeeper. The Opinion Creatures had heard William and understood well what he had said. Suddenly, the skies became filled with Opinion Creatures. There were so many of them the sky could not be seen! They were talking among themselves. One of the Opinion Creatures cried out loudly, "He means to destroy us all. We must destroy him first!"

All of the other Opinion Creatures began attacking the Gatekeeper. There were millions of these creatures, and they attacked in mass! The Gatekeeper was a strong and negative being but the numbers of these creatures were too much for him. The creatures were biting him and trying to rip him apart. They were on the Gatekeeper like bees on a hive.

"Stand down you fools, or I will destroy you all!" cried the Gatekeeper. However, there were too many creatures for him to stop and soon the creatures destroyed the Gatekeeper. The Opinion Creatures did not have to see the Gatekeeper. They could sense him. The view from the ship was frightening to William. He could see the creatures attacking what appeared to be a storm! The storm was the Gatekeeper. After a fierce battle, the Gatekeeper was no more! However, thousands of Opinion Creatures had been destroyed. When the lost souls in the Sea of Confusion saw the keeper gone and many dead creatures, they tried harder to get out of the sea, but Addictions would not loosen his hold on them. After the keeper was gone, the sky became a deep blue, and the sun shone brightly. Danielle thought to herself. "We have won a battle but not a war!" Negativity sees all and is everywhere! Negativity was very angry and shook the entire castle where Addictions was staying. In the Dark Land a voice came from everywhere. The voice was evil and thunderous, "King Addictions. Show yourself!"

Addictions came out of the castle and looked to the sky where the voice seemed to be coming from.

"Master, where are you if not in the pit!" shouted Addictions. The entire ground around the Dark King shook.

"Fool. I am everywhere and in everyone. The pit is but one place. I am everywhere at all times!" roared Negativity. King Addictions took the form of a black robe. Nothing else on the King was visible to the human eye. Addictions did not show his form. He chose to wear no face as to not be recognized.

"What troubles you my Dark Master?" shouted Addictions. No reply came right away. After what seemed like a long time, an answer finally came.

"You fool. You let pathetic humans defeat you. These humans are but children. If I did not still need your help, you would be cast into a hell that would torture even a being like you!" roared Negativity.

Once again the Dark Knight, Fear, turned on King Addictions. The Dark King looked toward the sky and shouted,

"Mercy. Oh, Dark Master. Surely I will make right this wrong!" Once again silence. After a long period of time, the evil and thunderous voice returned, "If you value your existence, you will make it right!"

Then...the voice was gone and King Addictions was very angry.

"For this William, you and your friends will die!" shouted Addictions.

For a short time on the Sea of Confusion, the lost souls were able to see the blue skies and sunlight and were even able to feel Hope. The poor lost souls finally had some relief from King Addictions. Imagine that, for a little amount of time, the entire earth was free from Addictions. There would be no Alcohol or Drug related crimes. There would be no more broken homes caused by Addictions. There would be no more sadness.

William and Danielle saw the torture that the lost souls were in and wept. "We will avenge you... We will avenge all of you. We will destroy King Addictions and set all of you lost souls free!" shouted William.

CHAPTER THIRTEEN

KING ADDICTIONS' REVENGE

Back at the castle in the Dark Land, King Addictions was sulking over the recent loss of the Gatekeeper. He was very angry and wanted revenge. Since King Addictions meeting with Negativity, his Dark Knight, Fear, was a regular visitor!

"The ancient Master, Negativity, will destroy you if you fail him again!" said Fear.

"Take leave of me!" screamed Addictions.

"The ancient Dark Master will torment your soul for eternity if you fail him again!" teased Fear as he settled in for the day to torment Addictions.

"Be gone Fear!" shouted Addictions.

"At this very moment, I am thinking of a way to get revenge on the two weak humans and their friend," shouted Addictions in his anger.

"Perhaps I can be of help to you, oh great King," offered Fear.

After a moment of silence Addictions replied, "Perhaps you can at that, my Dark Knight!"

"I am at your service always Dark King, for it is I who keep people afraid to face life without you," said Fear.

"Good. I will speak to Negativity and have him cloak you from Truth for a short period of time.During that time you will go on board the Vessel of Truth pretending to be a lost soul who has seen the light. Then you will set fire to the vessel and bring the girl Danielle too me!"

Fear cackled in excitement. Fear was always happy to inflict himself on every human he could.

"I will do as you wish Addictions. The pathetic humans are no match for me!" boasted Fear.

Fear took the form of a summer's wind and headed for the Vessel of Truth.

In the meantime, William was talking with Danielle and Zom on the Vessel of Truth.

"You see, it is possible to defeat the Forces of Darkness!" said William, who was feeling very indestructible at the moment.

"Do not act so proud," warned Zom.

"Are you not happy that we won a small victory?" asked William.

"Do not underestimate the strength of the Dark Forces. My people were also proud until Addictions destroyed our city and took the lives of many," Zom replied sadly.

"I would like to hear the whole story of what happened to your people," said William earnestly.

"You will. But now is not the time," answered Zom.

"He is right. We need to plan our next move," said Danielle, already feeling exhausted.

"Our next move is to continue sailing to the Land of the Dark and do battle with Addictions," replied William.

As the three friends were preparing to make their plans on how to defeat Addictions, a summer wind approached the vessel. The wind felt warm and inviting, and Danielle was disappointed when the summer wind ceased. She heard somebody calling for help. When the three friends found the owner of the voice, they saw another lost soul who made safe passage to the deck of the ship.

"I did not hear the voice of Truth tell me that another soul would make it on board this vessel," William thought to himself. Then again, I did not hear a warning from Truth either," thought William.

Little did William know that the reason he had heard nothing from Truth is because Negativity had blinded Truth long enough for Fear to do his work.

Fear was already on board the Vessel of Truth and could not be seen by the human eye. When his unsuspecting hosts went to gather him some food and see to his sleeping quarters for the trip, Fear decided to call on his old friend for help. Deceit was resting peacefully in the castle at the Dark Land when he heard a voice,

"Deceit... Deceit. It is I, your old friend, Fear, and you need to help me with my plans to destroy the Vessel of Truth," the voice said.

Now this did not surprise Deceit because all of the Dark Beings could talk to each other using only their thoughts. Deceit smiled wickedly when he heard the message sent to him from Fear.

"How might I help you Fear, my old friend?" replied Deceit.

"Come to the Sea of Confusion and possess the lost soul that has just climbed up on the deck of the Vessel of Truth," replied Fear.

"What shall I do after the lost soul is possessed by me?" Asked Deceit.

"Once you are on board this ship, I will guide you from there," said Fear.

Deceit did as he was told and possessed the soul on board the Vessel of Truth.

"Who are you?" William asked the lost soul, as he offered him a small plate of tasty dried fruits.

"I am a lost soul who has seen the Truth and am no longer confused," said Deceit, in a very sincere voice.

"I was not informed of your arrival." said William.

"I only know that I am saved," replied the lost soul.

William hesitated for a moment, but then chastised himself for not trusting their new guest. Would not Truth have warned them if this lost soul were their enemy?

"Very well, welcome aboard," William said in a very friendly voice.

CHAPTER FOURTEEN

DECEIT DOES HIS DIRTY WORK

When the evening arrived, the four shipmates went below deck to the map room to begin making their plans for when they reached the Land of the Dark. The lost soul possessed by Deceit insisted he was weary from his travels and asked if Danielle could show him to his sleeping quarters. As Danielle obliged, Deceit sent out a silent message.

"Fear...Fear. What shall I do next?"

"Set fire to the ship and take the girl captive," replied Fear.

Deceit asked Danielle if he might get another helping of the delicious dried fruit, and, although the girl was getting just a little upset with their guest and his wants, she was a good girl and went to do his bidding. While she was gone, Deceit locked the door of the map room and broke the key off in the lock from the outside. Deceit then went back to his quarters, and when Danielle returned with his food, he grabbed a lantern hanging on the wall and threw it on the floor.

Danielle gasped as a fire started. The oil from the lamp had splashed on the walls, and the flames hungrily licked up the walls. Danielle saw what the lost soul was doing, but was too late to stop him.

"Why are you doing this?" Danielle cried in a horrified voice.

"You humans are so ignorant and easy to fool!" cackled Deceit, still disguised as a lost soul.

"But I thought that you saw the Light of Truth?" asked Danielle, who was now in tears.

At this time the lost soul began to change its form. The lost soul was now becoming Deceit, and Danielle saw the hideous Being he truly was. Deceit had a human body, but the body had two heads. One of Deceit's heads was of a wise old man with white hair and looked very much as a king would look. The other head of Deceit was that of a horned creature with red burning eyes. His body was old and broken looking, and in the eyes of Deceit, one could see Hell.

"You are not a lost soul. What manner of creature are you?" Danielle was trembling in fear.

"I am, forever and have deceived humans since the beginning of time!" proclaimed the horned head of the being.

"Why are you here?" cried Danielle.

"I have come to destroy this ship and take you to King Addictions," answered Deceit.

"I would rather die than go with you!" Danielle shouted in defiance.

"I was hoping you would say that you pathetic human," said Deceit in an evil voice. The horned head of the creature laughed and looked toward Danielle as its eyes began to radiate red light from them.

"Deceit...Deceit. Kill not the girl for she belongs to Addictions!" said Fear with his mind.

At that point, Deceit stopped laughing and the red light grew dim. Deceit had no desire to get Addictions angry with him.

"I live in all humans. The wise side of me tells them to lie and deceive, and the other side of me inflicts misery and suffering!" said Deceit.

"I will never go with you!" Danielle repeated herself, squaring her shoulders and trying to hide her fear.

"You already belong to Fear.

I can feel him in your soul!" said Deceit.

"I will not feel Fear for it will only take me to Addictions!

"Foolish girl. I have traveled the outer reaches of reality for eternity and am older than time. You have no choice but to go with me and Fear," the horned head spoke.

Danielle ran for the door to get out of the room that was filled with smoke as the flames spread and were very close to devouring her. She cried as Deceit grabbed her and took her to the deck of the ship and jumped into the sea. Danielle was screaming as she struggled with Deceit. While in the sea, she continued to struggle, but Deceit was too strong for her. At this time, Fear took the form of a hurricane and caught both Danielle and Deceit up in its winds and headed for the Dark Land.

"Deceit...you have done well. You have claimed an innocent victim and set fire to the Vessel of Truth. King Addictions will be well pleased!" Fear announced, very pleased with his friend Deceit.

The Vessel of Truth was burning very fast, and William and Zom knew as the map room started to fill up with smoke, that the ship was on fire and they were in great danger.

"We must get out of this room!" shouted William.

When William realized the door was locked, he began beating on it and trying to break it down, but the door was too strong and would not give in. Between the smoke and the struggle to get the door open, William fainted. Zom was now thinking that he could survive in the water, however, he did not think that William would survive in the water in his present state. Zom could not figure out what had happened. All he knew was that they had to get off of the ship to survive! After a few minutes, the door to the room that Zom and William were in was on fire. The fire weakened the door enough for Zom to be able to kick it down. Outside of the door the entire bottom of the ship was on fire and burning fast! Zom was not going to leave William, so, he would either get him off the ship or die with him!

"Zom. It is I, Truth. I have been blinded by the ancient Dark Master, Negativity," spoke Truth.

"We are going to die soon!" Zom said in a fearful voice.

"You will not die, for you are chosen to do battle with Addictions," continued Truth.

Zom could feel Truth in his soul but could not see him.

"How can we escape from this burning ship, and where is the girl?" asked Zom.

"Listen, creature of the deep, take the human to your city under the Sea of Confusion, and I will see to it that he does not drowned in the sea and that you make it to your home alive!" said Truth

Zom knew if he did not follow Truth he would be lost. The ship was now sinking's still wanted to know what had happened to Danielle, but did not have time to think about it at the present. The flames were now in the map room, climbing the walls and burning the wood. Zom picked William up in his arms as the water started rushing in through a hole the fire had created. The creature of the deep kicked the burnt boards loose and jumped through the side of the ship with William in his arms. He then was in the sea itself and was waiting on Truth to guide him from there.

CHAPTER FIFTEEN

THE PEOPLE OF THE DEEP

The Vessel of Truth was engulfed in flames and sinking fast. The lost souls were too confused by the Opinion Creatures to know that, miles below them, was the City of Serenity. The lost souls were in the same sea as the City of Serenity, but would never find it!

William was starting to awake in Zoms arms when he noticed that he was under water! William began to panic's told him to hold his breath and help would be with them soon.

When the two shipmates were about fifty feet below the water, a huge protective bubble formed around them. Inside the bubble there was a dry place. The bubble had air to breathe. William took in a huge gulp of air and exhaled. Zom knew that this was the help that Truth promised. The spirit of Truth had left the vessel that was now on its way to the bottom of the sea. The bubble did not float on top of the sea but proceeded to go further down into the depths of the sea. Zom knew that the bubble was going to the City of Serenity that was his home.

"Where is Danielle?" asked William with a tired voice.

"I do not know, but I think she was taken by one of Addictions' Dark

Knights!" replied Zom

William was now very tired and sad.

"We must get her back!" William said in a frantic voice.

"We will find her soon, but now you must rest!" exclaimed Zom.

The bubble continued to go deeper and deeper into the sea. William saw many strange and beautiful kinds of sea life.

"How is it that I am so far under water, yet I am breathing air?" William asked in a shocked voice.

"You are being protected by Truth," replied Zom

"Why do we go further down into the sea?" asked William.

"We are going to my home, the City of Serenity," answered Zom.

"Where is your home?" William asked.

"My home is far under the sea in a place that no human can reach," replied Zom.

"Do the people of the City of Serenity know that we are coming?" inquired William.

"The Old One who is a very wise being has sensed our arrival and has talk to me with his mind. He says our coming has been written in his ancient Holy Book," said Zom.

"How is it that the Old One senses us from so far away?" asked William.

"The Old One senses all. He has been around since the beginning of time, and he

Taught us how to escape Addictions by moving into the sea!" said Zom.

"Does the Old One ever talk like humans?" asked William.

"The Old One comes from a race of people who lived centuries ago. The Old One is the only one left of his kind. His race believed that talking was cheap and used too easily for the purpose of hurting other beings," replied Zom.

"Has the Old One known of King Addictions since his birth?" asked William.

"The Old One knows many things which is why we need to go to the City of Serenity and speak with him!" exclaimed Zom.

As the bubble continued to go deeper, much of the sea life could be seen. The two companions could see sharks, whales and an occasional octopus. All of the sea life moved very gracefully in the sea The world under the sea was very peaceful and serene. The beauty of the sea was a welcome comfort to William and Zom who were weary from their meeting with Fear and Deceit.

Truth saw to it that the two battle weary friends had plenty to eat. The journey to the city of Serenity had already taken three days. William and Zom talked much about Danielle and how they would go about getting her back.

"How much further is the city?" asked William.

"It is at least another day's journey," replied Zom.

"Will we be able to see the city as we approach it?" William asked.

"The city is hidden far into an underground cave. It is not visible to the eye," said Zom.

"Then how will we find it?" asked William.

"We will find it!" assured Zom.

"But there are many underground caves in the sea. How will we find the right one?" asked William, who was now becoming somewhat panicked.

"That is true, but I have keen senses and will sense when we are near the right cave," replied Zom.

"Why did you leave land to move so far under water?" William asked.

"All I can tell you is that Addictions destroyed our city on land. The Old One will have to give you the details," replied Zom.

Down they went, further and further into the Sea. The confusion remained on the surface of the sea but far below was Serenity. The ancient Dark One, Negativity, feared the City of Serenity, because it was too close to the confusion on the top of the Sea. The Old One of the City of Serenity was a thorn in the side of Negativity, because the Old One knew too much about the darkness and what could destroy it! Negativity feared the Old One because the Old One knew things that even Negativity did not know!

Another day passed under the sea whiles the two companions still traveling in the bubble.Upon awakening from a sleep, William noticed that the bubble was now heading for an underwater mountain.

"Zom, wake up we are going to crash into a mountain," shouted William.

"Wh....what?" exclaimed Zom.

Zom was still half asleep when he looked out of the bubble and saw the mountain.

"It is the Mountain of Hope!" exclaimed Zom

"What is the Mountain of Hope?" asked William.

"It is the mountain where the cave to the City of Serenity exists!" said Zom, very happily.

"Then let us go into the cave and begin our journey to the City of Serenity," William said.

"Yes, I can sense the entrance to the cave now," Zom said.

The bubble which was acting on the thought waves from Zom, headed straight to the entrance of the cave. The Mountain of Hope was huge and very far under the sea. It appeared to be on fire, but it was not on fire. It was just very bright."How long must we travel through the cave to get to the city?" inquired William?

"The cave is very long and the journey will take at least two days," answered Zom.

About ten miles into the cave, William was looking into the darkness of the cave when the cave was suddenly filled with a bright blue light.

"What is happening?" William asked, very startled

"Do not fear the light. It is the Light of Truth lighting the way to the City of Serenity," replied Zom.

CHAPTER SIXTEEN

DECEIT RETURNS TO FINISH THE JOB

On the journey through the cave, the Light of Truth was constant. On the second day of the journey through the cave, the light was gone.

"The light has gone!" cried William.

"I do not know why the light is gone, but I do not like it," said Zom.

Suddenly, another light appeared in the cave, but this light was an eerie green light. From the bowels of the cave, a creature began to stir. It could not be seen at first, but from the way the cave shook, it had to be very large.

The creatures movement caused the bubble to been thrown about like a toy. The creature arising from the bowels of the cave was Deceit in another form. It had taken the form of a huge octopus. At least, its body was that of an octopus. Its face was that of a tortured soul. Suddenly, the water in the cave was calm and the bubble came to a stop!

"What was that!" cried William.

"I do not know!" replied Zom.

Suddenly, the creature appeared in front of the bubble. It was huge and could have easily smashed the bubble to pieces. Shortly after it appeared in front of the bubble, it attached itself to a wall of the cave and slithered its way around the bubble. The tentacles of the octopus attached to the bubble and held it in place while the head of the creature looked into the bubble.

"What manner of creature is this?" asked Zom.

"It is unlike anything I have ever seen!" replied William.

The creatures face appeared to be distorted. It had long dark hair and a beard both of which looked very shabby. The creature's mouth was open and appeared as the mouth of a dead man. The teeth of the creatures were black and rotting.

"Turn back. The side you fight on is the wrong one," spoke the creature.

The creature's mouth stayed the same yet the words issued forth from it.

"Be gone creature, and let us continue our journey!" shouted William.

"What you believe is not the Truth," bellowed the creature.

"What do you know of the Truth?" asked Zom.

"In the beginning there was darkness. Then the darkness created the light, and in the end there will be only darkness," spoke the creature.

"Do not listen to the creature Zom, for it is Deceit!" warned William.

"There is nothing good and Heaven does not exist. Darkness and death are real. You must take anything you can to feel good now," bellowed the creature.

Once again, Zom was falling into confusion. He held his ears and let out a painful cry!

"The creature of the deep knows that I speak the Truth. If you want any kind of a good life then you will listen to me William," spoke the creature.

"You are lying, creature. I have had many good feelings and many good people have helped me and surely there is a life after death!" cried William.

"Yes, human. There is a life after death. It is called Hell!" said the creature in a mocking voice.

"The feeling I get when the stars are out at night, or when a friend comforts me in my suffering, and remembering all of the warm summer days and the happy times in my life, that is what people remember the easiest," said William.

"Acts of kindness are what people never forget." finished William in a determined voice.

"Deceit...Deceit...The boy speaks the truth, and you speak nothing but lies," spoke the voice of Truth into the mind of Deceit.

Deceit screamed in agony. The scream was so powerful that it shook the walls of the cave.

"Be gone, Truth, for you have no business here!" screamed Deceit.

Once again, the blue light began to fill the cave. The light was brighter than before. The blue light began to enter into Deceit's body.

"I am filled with the light of Truth, and soon I will perish, but I will be back. For I am immortal!" shouted Deceit, in agony.

The blue light began breaking up the body of the creature, and soon the body of the creature exploded.

The body of the creature was gone, but the voice of Deceit continued for a short time.

"The Truth does not exist. To humans anything is the truth, and to them, as long as it gets them what they want, (even if it is false), they swear it is the truth!" said Deceit, as his voice finally faded away.

"William...Zom...It is I, Truth, the Dark Knight. Deceit is very powerful and appears to speak the truth, but, in the end, Truth will win out over Deceit," spoke Truth, into the minds of William and Zom.

"How will we know if it is you or Deceit?" asked Zom.

"You will know Deceit by its end results. The only thing that can come from Deceit is pain and misery." Truth answered.

CHAPTER SEVENTEEN

WILLIAM AND ZOM REACH THE CITY OF SERENITY

Not long after the battle with Deceit, William and Zom were able to see the City of Serenity at a distance. The gates of the city were made of blue crystal, and stood ten stories high. On the side of the gates were watchtowers made of blue crystal and in the towers were two beings who looked much like Zom. As the bubble drew nearer the city, the two guards in the watchtower blew large horns made of seashells the horns were very loud and were to alert the city that a vessel was approaching it. At the very front of the gate there swam a huge white shark. The shark was the protector of the gate.

"Atlas, my home is in sight!" exclaimed Zom, very happily.

"I have never seen a gate so big!" exclaimed William.

As the bubble approached the gate, Zom sent a telepathic signal to the huge shark, and the shark swam away from the gate to allow the bubble entry. The huge crystal gates opened and the bubble containing Zom and William entered into the City of Serenity.

At first sight, William saw skyscrapers made of blue crystal and some other buildings that were made of clear crystal. The sight was unbelievably beautiful. The City of Serenity had streets made of ground up seashells and vehicles that appeared to run on water for fuel.

Many beings appeared to use boats to travel the city. The boats were made of wood and beautifully crafted. As the bubble approached the center of the city, many beings stopped to see whom they were that were landing in their city in a bubble. While floating towards the center of the city, William saw a statue that was huge.

"Who does that statue honor?" asked William.

"The statue honors the wise man of our city," answered Zom.

When the bubble landed in the center of the city, Zom and William got out of the bubble. Some of the beings recognized Zom and greeted him. Others were just curious.

"Come my friend, we must go to a place that will give us shelter for the night, and I know of just the place," said Zom, grabbing William by the arm and moving quickly out of the crowd of beings.

While finally being able to slow down a bit, Zom let go of Williams arm and told William to follow him. While walking down a back street of the city, William had a chance once again to look around. William felt a wave of serenity hit him and all of the good times in William's life flooded back into his memory and filled him with peace.

"Where are we going?" asked William.

"We are going to see a friend of mine who owns a factory that builds the boats used in this city to take my people where they wish to go!" answered Zom.

Back and forth the beings of the city went about their business. All of the beings appeared happy. The City of Serenity was at peace with life. Wars and crime did not exist in the City of Serenity, and the beings of the city believed that peace was easily had if all of the beings believed in it. Each and every being in the city was considered very important, and their feelings were looked upon as sacred. The city had air that was breathable by humans and the beings of the deep alike. It was a city that lived through the worst and worked towards the best possible life it could have. The beings of the City of Serenity were the survivors of the invasion of King Addictions. They had all lost loved ones, and to them life was the most important gift of all!

Zom and William reached the factory in an hour's spotted his friend working outside in the boat yard.

"Yem, my friend, it is I, Zom!" shouted Zom, very happily.

"Zom. I thought you dead at the hands of King Addictions!" exclaimed Yem.

"I was saved by the being, Truth, and my friend here, who is called William," replied Zom.

"It must be a good sign. Nobody has ever returned from the Sea of Confusion," said Yem.

"We are going to the Dark Land to do battle with King Addictions," said William, in a serious voice.

"Have you taken leave of your senses?" asked Yem.

"No, my friend, we still have our senses and we seek to destroy Addictions," answered Zom.

"You will need the help of the Old One," said Yem.

"I will speak with the Old One, for he knows many things about the ancient ones," replied Zom.

"Very well, my friends. Then come into my factory and let me show you around. Afterwards we can go to my home and have some dinner!" said Yem.

William and Zom were very happy to accept the offer for dinner for they were very hungry. After seeing the factory, Yem took them to his house, which was right next to the factory. The dinner was huge. Yem had prepared all kinds of seafood for the two weary companions. William and Zom ate much food. Then the three of them went into Yem's living room to talk

"There is a meeting tonight at the city hall. I think you should go and listen to some of the beings talk about what they know of Addictions," said Yem.

"Yes, we would like to go," said William.

William and Zom spent most of the day with Yem. Afterwards, Zom found them a boat and they headed for the meeting at the city hall.

"How does the sunlight get into your city?" asked William.

"The crystal dome that covers the city draws the sunlight from above the ground and channels it into our city," replied Zom.

"Why is it that I can breathe air this far below the sea?" inquired William.

"This city has many caves which reach up to the surface. The air comes through the caves and down in our city," replied Zom.

The boat left the dock carrying William and Zom on it. The boat was sailing on smooth water and William had a chance to take another look at the city. The buildings in the city were very tall and had many stories to them. Some of the businesses that William saw were businesses that were a service to the beings of the city. All of the Beings on the streets appeared to be very helpful to one another.

There were food businesses, construction businesses and many other types of institutions. William saw that the buildings were all made of crystal. Some were clear crystal and others were blue and green crystal.

After sailing on the boat for about an hour, the building they were going to was in sight. It was a clear crystal building and had only three stories to it. The people in the building could be seen from the outside. It looked like there were humans and people of the deep together.

"Where are all of the humans coming from?" asked William, in an excited voice.

"You need to know that we were once human, and so we work with other humans toward a common good which is to fight Addictions," replied Zom.

CHAPTER EIGHTEEN

THE TOWN HALL MEETING

The boat docked and William and Zom left the boat and went to the building where the meeting was being held. They went to the third floor where the meeting was and found that it had already started. While at the meeting they heard many stories of how these beings were able to escape King Addictions. They also spoke of the friends and family they had lost to King Addictions. William listened to the stories and felt a great sadness for the beings telling the stories and for the loss of his soul mate, Danielle.

WILLIAM, ZOM MEET VOLA AND THE OLD ONE

One of the beings spoke from the crowd.
"I heard from one of the other beings that you and Zom are on a quest to destroy King Addictions," the Being said.
"It is true. We seek to destroy Addictions," replied William.

"I would like to join you in your quest," the being said.

"Who are you, and why do you want to join our quest?" Zom inquired.

"My name is Vola and King Addictions destroyed my entire family," answered the being in an angry voice.

"You have no idea of what we are up against. We could easily be destroyed!" exclaimed William.

"I no longer care how powerful King Addictions is. He has destroyed my entire family and the city we lived in," said Vola in an angry voice.

Vola was a creature like Zom, and he was of the same race.

"We used to be beings of the land and only played in the sea at our leisure until Addictions came to our land and forced us to flee for our souls." said Vola.

"He saw the same horrors as I did," said Zom in a sad voice.

"Very well then, he can join us!" exclaimed William.

The meeting continued for a better part of the evening. After a few hours the meeting began to end. Soon the only ones left were William, Zom and Vola.

"We must sleep now. We need to be up early to visit the Old One of Serenity," said Zom.

"Yes, the wise man will tell us of a cave that reaches all the way up to the ground. The only cave that will take us to the Dark Land!" exclaimed Vola.

So, the three warriors left the meeting hall and were welcomed into Vola's home for the evening. Once they arrived at the home of Vola they were shown by Vola where they could sleep for the night.

The three friends were very tired and morning came fast. Vola was up before the others and had breakfast waiting for William and Zom.

Breakfast consisted of eggs and fish. The fish were from the sea and William and Zom found the fish to be very tasty.

They also had a very delicious drink that was equal to the human drink called orange juice.

After breakfast, Vola packed up some supplies and headed for the front door of his home.

"Come my friends. We must leave to see the Old One!" exclaimed Vola.

The Old One lived under the statue in the center of town. A door existed at the bottom of the statue that opened onto a stairway. The stairway led far under the City of Serenity.

The three warriors left Vola's house and began their walk through the city. On their way they walked through several small streets and past many other homes. When William and his friends reached the door at the bottom of the statue, they stopped. Zom sent certain signals out from his mind, and the door opened. Once the door was opened, they all began to walk down the stairway.

"The door was sealed tight. How did you get it opened?" asked William.

"I talked to the Old One with my mind and told him who we were and what our quest is." replied Zom.

The stairway seemed to be an endless journey for the three comrades. On the way down the stairway they saw many paintings. The paintings were of nowhere land in happier days before King Addictions took root. Once the three warriors arrived at the bottom of the stairway. The sea was there to greet them.

"Have we walked this far under the city just to end up at the sea?" asked William.

"This is not the sea. This is but an illusion," replied Zom.

Zom sat down on the bottom step and concentrated on the sea. After concentrating on the sea for a few minutes. The sea vanished and another set of stairs appeared.

"Why were we tricked into believing that this was the sea?" asked William.

"Many times in this life, things are not what they seem to be," answered Zom.

"What do you mean?" asked William.

"Sometimes it is wise to take a second look at something so you can see it in a different light," explained Zom.

This set of stairs went down three more flights and ended at a large chamber that was very dark inside. When the three warriors entered the chamber a bright blue light illuminated the chamber. Sitting on a throne in the middle of the chamber was the Old One. The Old One had beard and eyes that looked as if they had seen centuries of life. The ancient one was only about five foot tall and was holding a staff that was made of wood. The staff was white on the top and black on the bottom. The ancient one gazed on them as if he could see right through them.

"What is it that you seek?" the ancient asked..

"We seek wisdom," replied William.

"You have found wisdom," replied the ancient one.

"What happened to the city above ground where your people once lived?" inquired William.

"We were once a very highly advanced people. The most advanced in the land, but try as we might, we could not find the technology to master our emotions." said the Old One.

"How did that destroy your city?" William asked.

"We were thinking so much about technology and material things that we never took time to think about how we were feeling on a daily basis," replied the wise man.

The Old One continued, "We spent so much time praising ourselves that we never tried to figure out why we were so unhappy. Our people became so wrapped up in all of the great things we created, and the fact that we had anything we needed, that we threw away our emotions and had only pure logic, but more than logic is needed when a being has a soul!"

"Do you mean that you never felt love or happiness?" asked William.

"We became selfish and vain and thought that we did not need emotion. We thought we could just forget our emotions and live on logic," replied the Old One.

"Did you just live on logic?" asked William.

"We tried to live on nothing but logic, and we became emotionally void and miserable. That is when King Addictions came around offering the people of our city a way to escape the misery by taking his magic potions!" exclaimed the Old One.

"That was the beginning of the end for our city above ground," said Zom, in an angry voice.

"All of our people started using the potions at first for relief from stress and worry, then before too long our people found that they could not quit taking the potions!" exclaimed the Old One.

"Did you try to talk sense to them about what Addictions was doing to them?" asked William.

"Yes, the ones that did not follow Addictions tried to talk sense into the others, but it was too late. By then no logic existed," spoke the Old One.

"Our rate of crime grew, and people were dying of strange illnesses. Our technology was at a stop and insanity ruled our city, so the scientists that were left and not following Addictions, decided it was time to leave the city and seek refuge under the sea where we would not have to live with Addictions," said the Old One.

"The scientists that were left took all of the known technology and applied it to building this very city we are now in!" exclaimed Zom."

"Then our scientists took all of our survivors and transformed their bodies to survive in and under water," said the Old One.

"So the beings who came here with you are saved from King Addictions?" inquired William.

"No. Not saved. The ones who were still alive and came with us still hear the voice of Addictions in their heads. They can never escape Addictions, but they can stop using the magic potions and be happy once again," answered the Old One.

"How can they ever be happy if they can never get Addictions out of their minds?" asked William.

"When these beings hear Addictions calling for them, they call on the help of another being who is suffering from the same problem. The person with the same problem talks to them and tells them what they did to avoid going back to the magic potions," answered the Old One.

"Then, there is hope!" exclaimed William.

"Yes, there is always hope. The people afflicted with Addictions form groups to help each other," said the Old One.

"We must go then, to defeat King Addictions as soon as we can!" exclaimed William.

"No! You do not understand. King Addictions is not of this world.He travels through time in the souls of humanity hidden from conscious thought, and he calls on negative beings to do his bidding. If Addictions were of this world, then people could defeat him with rational thought!" spoke the Old One.

"Do you mean that its secret is that it is invisible to the human eye?" asked Zom.

"Yes, he travels in a world that is ancient, and he was here long before humans," spoke the Old One.

"The Old One thought for a moment and then said,"

"The only way to hold Addictions at bay is to have some kind of awakening. Once an awakening happens, then the being, seeing that Addictions is real, can begin to fight."

"We must take our chances and go to the Dark Land to do battle with Addictions or all will be lost anyway," said William.

"Many of the people who have formed these groups here in the city believe that the power which can defeat Addictions is Truth," said the Old One.

"We must go now. Our journey will be hard," said Vola.

"The path you seek to the Dark Land exists here in my chamber - just behind my throne is a cave. Take the cave up to the surface to reach the dark land, and may Truth be with all three of you," finished the Old One.

ENTERING THE CAVE AND BEGINNING THE JOURNEY

The three warriors then entered the cave and began their journey. The cave was dark and treacherous, and Vola brought torches for lighting the way. There were no encounters with Negative Beings in the cave, but the cave went straight to the surface, and there were steep mountain-like rocks to be climbed. It would take three days of travel in the cave to reach the Dark

Land. On the first day of travel our three would-be heroes talked amongst themselves about all of the things that have change since the coming of King Addictions.

During their time in the cave, they were climbing steep rocks and camping on whatever flat land they could find, but the wise Old One always remained on their minds during their journey.

"We will make it to the Dark Land, but will we survive what lies in wait for us?" asked Vola.

"I would rather die fighting than to be one of the walking dead whose soul belongs to Addictions," said William.

"You are right my friend. Those who walk with Addictions live in constant fear, and when they try to escape from Addictions, they are cast into emotional turmoil," said Zom.

"I cannot help but worry about my friend, Danielle. Where is she?Is she alive? Does her soul still belong to her?" asked William in a sad way.

"Worry not my friend. We will find Danielle, for she is a person of Truth and no harm will come to her!" exclaimed Zom.

"I never should have let her come with me on this journey," said William, regretfully.

"If she had not gone with you, she would have been prey for anyone of the Negative Beings, and she would have been and outcast from the world," said Zom.

"She is in the captivity of Addictions. How can anything be worse than that?" asked William.

"She is in the captivity of Addictions, but she is a child of Truth, and King Addictions would not dare harm her!" exclaimed Zom.

The journey in the cave continued and the closer they got to the Dark Land, the more determined they became to destroy Addictions.

CHAPTER NINETEEN

THE VILLAGE OF BACKWARDS

N ow, on the coast that lay on the Dark Side of the Land of Nowhere, there stood another village that existed unscathed by the influence of Addictions. Life for the people of this particular village was totally backwards from any other village in nowhere land. For instance, in Backwards, people were born old and passed into the next life as an infant. The younger a person was, the wiser they were.

When the Village of Backwards was visited by Addictions, instead of becoming addicted, the people of Backwards became un-addicted. This made Addictions very angry, but he was powerless to do anything about it.

Like many of the other villages, the Village of Backwards had a gatekeeper. His name was Jeremiah, a young child who took his responsibility to stand against any Dark Forces wishing entrance into his beloved village very seriously.

William and his friends made it out of the cave and away from the land under the sea. The Village of Backwards was only a few miles up the road from where the caves exit existed, and after walking a couple of miles, William spotted the Village of Backwards.

"Look. it is a village. We can rest there!" exclaimed William very tired from the journey.

"Wait. How do we know that the village is not full of Dark Beings?" asked Vola.

"We do not know, but let us go up to the village and find out. If it is a Dark village, we will seek rest out in the woods," said Zom, who was tired of talking and needing rest..

Very tired from their struggles, the three warriors all seemed to agree with this idea and proceeded to walk up to the entrance of the Village of Backwards. When the three warriors reached the gate they were surprised to see a lone child with dark hair guarding the gate.

"Hello, little one," William said to the child. "May we speak to the gatekeeper?"

"I ma eht erpeeketag, dna ohw era uoy?" inquired Jeremiah.

"What did he say?" asked William, in an exhausted voice.

Now in the past, Zom had met some people from the Village of Backwards and had learned some of their customs and language that, like everything else in the village, was backwards.

Zom explained the way things were in the Village of Backwards to William and Vola.

William and Vola felt relieved, because they thought they were both going crazy. "He said, "I am the gatekeeper, and who are you?" interpreted Zom.

"Tell him that we have journeyed from far below the earth, and we have been chosen to do battle with King Addictions," said William, still fearful of the battle ahead.

Zom told the gatekeeper what William had said.

"woh nac enoyna od elttab htiw "snoitciddA" dna evivrus?" asked Jeremiah, who was looking at the three warriors like they had lost their minds.

"He asked how anybody can do battle with Addictions," interpreted Zom.

"Tell him we can do battle with Addictions and survive with the help of the Positive Beings," said William, who was beginning to wander if he would even make it into the village.

"fI uoy lliw pleh su, ew osla evah ytevitisoPgnipleh su, ew knith ew dnats a ecnahc," said Zom in Jeremiah's language

Jeremiah, who was sitting with his back towards William and his friends, thought a moment and said,

"I tsum klat ot eht rehto elpoep fo eht egalliv tsrif,"

I asked him for the help of the village. He said that he must talk to the other Beings in the village first," Zom told his friends.

At this point, Jeremiah began walking backwards into his village.

"Do you think the village will agree to help us?" asked Vola, who was missing the sea.

"If they do not, we will still fight Addictions ourselves!" exclaimed William, growing a little impatient with the child.

Our three comrades knew they could gain much knowledge from this village.

When Jeremiah returned, he told William and his friends that his village was willing to help them. Upon entering the village, William and his friends were amazed to see the village people walking backwards.

All the people of the village appeared to be happy, despite the fact that they lived on the Dark Side of the land.

There was an old man sitting on a fountain in the village square chanting, "What can be done, can be undone."

Jeremiah, who was a young child with deep, piercing blue eyes and coal black hair, began to speak to William and his friends,

"Gnithyreve tahtyetevitageNdeirt ot yortsed su htiw edam su regnorts,"

Zom then interpreted the words of Jeremiah.

"Jeremiah says that everything Negativity tried to destroy us with only made us stronger."

Zom went on to explain to his friends that every evil thing that Addictions put on the Village of Backwards was reversed and turned into good.

Jeremiah then went on to explain that what makes Addictions so hard to beat is the fact that Addictions is not from this world.

So, what you are saying is that Addictions cannot be destroyed?" asked William, in a trembling voice.

Jeremiah says that the only thing that can destroy Addictions is bringing him out into the open and proving that he really does exist!" interpreted Zom.

Suddenly, the old man in the village square began chanting in a much louder voice,

"What has been done, can be undone...what has been done, can be undone." The old man's voice echoed off the mountains that surrounded the village.

"erehT si eno ohw nac yortsed snoitciddA rof doog, emos llac eht gneib dog, emos llca ti erutan, emos od ton eveileb eht gneib tsixe," spoke Jeremiah.

"Jeremiah says that there is one who can destroy Addictions for good. Some call the being, God. Others call it Nature.Some do not believe the being exists." interpreted Zom.

The old man chanting in the square then began to speak.

"You have good feelings, yet you cannot see them, but you can feel them, so you know they exist. If you believe in the great wizard called God then the being does exist."

The entire village grew silent. Everyone in the village thought about what the old man had said, and it made sense. Immediately after the old man chanted out the wisdom about belief, he went back to chanting the same thing which he chanted every day and night.

"What can be done, can be undone," the old man continued to chant.

"I have heard of this being. It is said that only powerful Positive Beings can summons the great Wizard," said Vola.

"Then we must call on one of the Positive Beings to summons the great God that they speak of!" exclaimed William.

"How will you summons this Positive Being?" inquired Vola.

William was already erasing the negative thoughts from his mind and thinking about only things that are good. Suddenly, a great white light appeared in the village square right next to the old man. It was the being, Love, and it took the form of a great white light.

"Greetings to the people of Backwards and to the brave warriors who are destined to do battle with Addictions," spoke Love.

"Greetings to you, Love, and thank you for coming," said William who stood in awe of this Being.

"Why do you call on me?" Love asked.

"We need you to summons the great wizard," said William.

"I can summons this being, but I will need your help. The entire village must erase all thoughts from their minds and think of only good things. This is the only way to summons the being you speak of," said Love.

"You heard what the being has said. Everybody - think of only good things!" shouted William.

CHAPTER TWENTY

THE VILLAGE OF BACKWARDS SUMMONS THE WIZARD

At this point, the entire village began erasing all bad thoughts from their minds and thought of only good. The entire village began to feel good. There was not one being in the village that needed drugs or alcohol to feel good. They just naturally felt good. Each one of the beings had the ability to feel good inside of them. The beings of the village did not rely on what others said or did for they're happiness.

When all of the Beings of the village were thinking only good thoughts, they created a powerful feeling throughout the Land of Nowhere. During this time, the land became full of light and goodness. This caused the Dark Beings to tremble in fear and hide in the deepest, darkest places they could find.Suddenly, out of the West, came a mass of huge white clouds. The clouds stationed themselves over the Village of Backwards and began to take on the form of a giant old Wizard dressed in a white robe and standing at least a hundred feet tall.

The Wizard had stars for eyes and his long white robe had stars scattered all over it.The clouds, now shaped as a Wizard, looked down upon the Village of Backwards and asked in a roaring voice,

"Who summons me from the Realm of the Good?"

"eW eht elpoep fo sdrwkcab snommus uoy," replied Jeremiah.

The wizard needed no interpretation, for it was He who created all of the languages.

"Why do you summons me?" asked the Wizard in a thunderous voice.

"We intend to do battle with Addictions and need your help," pleaded William in a humble voice.

"My son, Positivity, has visited me and told me of his dark brother's work, said the Wizard

"Negativity has been in existence since before the beginning of time," continued the Wizard.

"Has he any weaknesses?" asked Zom very fearfully.

"Weakness does not exist in the Realm of the Good. The things of my realm are of a spiritual nature, and spirits have no form except the form they choose at the time they wish to show themselves," spoke the Wizard.

"How can we defeat a spirit?" asked Vola, becoming frustrated.

"Addictions cannot be defeated, because he is part of my dark son's soul. When the time comes, I will tell you how to defeat him," spoke the Wizard.

"When were you created?" William asked the Wizard.

"I have never been created but have always been and will always be," answered the Wizard.

"First, I created your world. Then the beings of your world called me their God. After that, they began to call themselves God, making it easy for my dark son to deceive them," finished the Wizard.

The Wizard then took on the form of the mass of clouds and began to journey back to the Land Of The Good. After the clouds were a few miles away a thunderous voice spoke so loud that the whole land could hear it

"When the time comes, seek me out in the Land Of The Good!" roared the Wizard.

"Tonight we meet at the Village Inn and put together our plan of battle!" said William who was tired and in need of rest.

When night fell on the land, all of the beings of Backwards met at the Village Inn to take part in the planning of the attack on King Addictions.

In the Realm of the Good, all of the Positive Beings were dawning their armor and weapons preparing for the spiritual battle against Addictions.

In the Realm of the Bad, all of the beings were preparing for a spiritual battle with the Positive Beings.

The Wizard would be the planner of the battle against the Dark Beings, and Positivity would be the high commander who leads the White Knights in battle.

Negativity would be the planner of the battle against the Positive Beings and Addictions would be the high commander.

At the inn in the Village of Backwards, all of the beings were now present and the meeting began.

"How will we travel to the castle of Addictions without being seen?" inquired Vola.

"We cannot go unseen. We must prepare ourselves for attacks aimed at us from Negative Beings. All of Hell knows that we are trying to destroy Addictions, and they hate us and will seek to destroy us!" answered William.

"Will we be the only ones attacking the Dark Armies?" inquired Zom in a very fearful voice.

"No. We will be in battle with many other Positive Beings some of which will help us," answered William.

"I tnaw ot og oot!" exclaimed Jeremiah.

"Jeremiah says that he wants to go with us," interpreted Zom.

"My friends. How brave you are and what good friends you are. You know, as well as I do, that we all stand to be killed in this battle, but you still stand by my side," said William, in a proud voice.

At that point, Vola shouted at the top of his voice,

Better to die fighting Addictions then to rot away under his influence."

Following the words spoken by Vola, all of the beings at the Inn stood up and began cheering then they began to shout in unison,

"Long may live the Realm of the Good. And long live the people of nowhere land!"

Suddenly, tears came to William's eyes. He cried for the way things were before Addictions took root and for all the good people lost to Addictions. He then looked upon the crowd of people at the Inn and shouted,

"Death to King Addictions, and death to all of his Evil Beings!"

All the people from the Village of Backwards who were at the meeting began to shout,

"Life to King Addictions, and life to his Evil Beings,"

Of course, everything in the Village of Backwards means the opposite, so it was not life they were wishing for King Addictions or his Knights.

"We must continue the meeting now," shouted William.

"So, the four of us will travel on foot to the dark castle of King Addictions and seek him out and destroy him," said Zom.

"We will have the aid of the Positive Beings, but we will still be in much danger," said Vola, who was angry just thinking about Addictions.

"We must find Danielle before we do anything else!" exclaimed William.

"Yes. He is right. We must first save our friend Danielle!" exclaimed

Zom.

"In the end nothing can come from Negativity except Positivity," said William.

"I am not sure what that means," said Vola, with a confused look on his face.

"Then, let me explain," Said William.

William looked out onto the beings, which came for the meeting, and said,

"If there were no day, than night would have no meaning. And if there were no sadness then happiness would mean nothing. For everything that exists, there is an opposite. When life becomes out of balance it seeks to restore the balance.

"What does this have to do with Negativity?" asked Vola.

"It has everything to do with Negativity. When things are out of balance and things are too dark, life will find a way to even things out again," answered William.

"What is life?" asked Zom

"Some think that all of life is a dream or illusion. Life is real. But there are some illusions in life. King Addictions uses the illusions to make beings think they need his magic potions to be happy, but, in the end, they bring only misery and death," said William.

"Why do the beings that are addicted keep using the magic potions?" asked Vola.

"Because when they want to quit using the magic potions, Denial steps in and tells them that they have no problem, and if they want to be happy, they need to keep using the magic potions," answered William, in an angry voice.

"Jeremiah says that the emotions are attached to the soul, and if Addictions owns your soul, he owns your emotions," said Zom.

"Tomorrow, before the sun rises, my three friends and I will begin our journey deep into the Dark Side of the land to do battle with King Addiction. If we should fail remember the truth about Alcohol and Drugs. They are Negative Beings, who wear the mask of Positive Beings, but they can be seen by their results, and they are pain and sadness," said William

With this, William rested and gathered his thoughts. Once he had gathered his thoughts, he began speaking again,

"Since Positivity is the opposite of Negativity, we must seek to find a balance in life and bring back more good to our world,"

After the meeting, Jeremiah insisted that his friends stay at his house until they started out for their battle in the early morning hours. Our three friends were happy to stay at Jeremiah's house but it was confusing since everything in the house was built backwards.

Aggie paused for a moment from her tale. Then she took Danny's hand and said,

"You see, my sleeping friend, William knew that good feelings just like bad feelings could be recalled, because even in the darkest of all places, the Light of Goodness shines through and can be called on."

Danny was, for the most part, a wandering, unseen soul floating along with William and his friends.

"I see that you understand this Danny, so let's get back to nowhere land," said Aggie.

While staying at Jeremiah's home for the evening, Jeremiah told the other three comrades about the land that they would be traveling on the next day. What the other three comrades did not know was that there were many mountains in the Dark Land and that the castle of King Addictions was on top of the highest mountain in the Dark Side of the land!

After listening to Jeremiah talk of the mountains, William told the others that they needed to pack some food and warm clothing along with ropes for the trip.

Jeremiah told the others that they needed to get some sleep before the trip so they all retired for the night.

CHAPTER TWENTY-ONE

BEGINNING THE JOURNEY UP
THE MOUNTAIN

William told the people of the village that he and his friends would up before the sun all packed and ready to go. Soon the four friends were on the road out of the Village of Backwards.

The road was made of dirt but was flat and easy to travel. When they had traveled two hours on the road, William noticed that the land was becoming rougher and very hilly. After four hours of travel, the comrades were in the foothills of a mountain.

"This mountain looks like it goes all the way to the stars!" exclaimed Zom, who was looking up the side of the mountain.

After saying this, Zom noticed that he was talking to the back of Jeremiah's head. "Turn around so I can see your face Jeremiah!" said Zom, very frustrated. Jeremiah did not understand. He was, after all, standing in his natural way. After a while of talking to Jeremiah's head, Zom decided to just go around to the other side of Jeremiah so he could speak to him face to face. "If this mountain leads to the castle of Addictions, then we must make the climb, no matter how hard it will be," said Zom.

So our four friends started climbing the mountain. At the end of the first day they camped out on the side of the mountain. It was a quiet night and the stars shone so brightly they looked like diamonds in the sky. They made a fire and cooked up some food they had brought with them. Afterwards, they sat around drinking hot coffee and talking.

"I do not like this one bit. We have not had any problems up to now and to me that does not seem right," exclaimed Vola, fearing a trap around every corner.

"xaleR, ro dluow uoy ekil em ot dnif emos smelborp rof ouy?"Jeremiah asked.

"Jeremiah told you to relax or would you like him to find some problems for you?" said Zom.

Jeremiah was a five-year-old child but very wise. He not only walked well, but he walked very good when he was walking backwards.

"Jeremiah is right. There will be many problems on the road ahead. Until then, let's get some rest," said William, growing impatient with his friends bickering.

The night went on until morning with no problems. The four comrades packed their things and started up the mountain. Farther up the mountain, William and his friends traveled through snow and freezing temperatures. During these times they kept the fire blazing at night and talked among themselves. The following day, they would encounter the first being on their journey. During the following day they were traveling up the mountain when they thought they heard a voice on the wind.

"Did you hear that?" inquired Zom.

"Hear what?" asked Vola.

"I heard it too!" said William.

THE ENCOUNTER WITH THE MAN IN THE RUT

It was a brisk day and the sky was clear and deep blue. Suddenly, a shout for help caught the attention of the four travelers.

"It is coming from the north, up a little farther on the mountain in that wooded area!" exclaimed Zom.

"Come on, lets go see who it is!" said William.

At that point they all headed up the mountain toward the small wooded area to the north. When they got there they saw a being that appeared to be human, like William. The human was stuck in the ground. They were all surprised to see that the being was stuck in the ground up to his waist

"What are you doing in the ground?" asked Vola.

"What does it look like? I'm in a rut!" exclaimed the man in an angry voice.

"I have never seen a person stuck in a rut," said William.

"Well, I have never seen two creatures like the ones you are with, nor have I seen a child who walks backwards," answered the man in the rut.

"That is a good point. So, how did you get in a rut?" asked William.

"I was on my way to get my soul back from King Addictions when I started thinking about how impossible it would be to take my soul back from Addictions. I fell in a rut and have been here every since," said the man in the rut.

While the man in the rut was speaking, a Dark Knight appeared in the form of a beautiful woman. The woman had dark hair and deep blue eyes.

The woman walked up to William and said,

"Leave the man in the rut, and leave this place,"

"What if we wish to free him?" asked William.

"If you free him, he will turn on you and kill all of you!" exclaimed the woman.

Jeremiah had a feeling that he knew this being, which was in the form of a woman. Jeremiah began walking towards the woman, and the woman appeared to become fearful at the sight of Jeremiah.

"Stop where you are, child. Come no closer!" said the woman.

Jeremiah continued to walk toward the woman.

"You are the being, called Deceit." Zom interpreted for Jeremiah.

"You area very wise child of Backwards," spoke the woman.

"What do you want from us?" asked William.

"I want you to know that you are all going to die, all of you. It has already been foretold!" screamed the woman.

The Evil Being, Deceit, knew that if Jeremiah touched him, he would become his opposite, which would be Truth. As Jeremiah moved closer to the woman, the woman left the ground and took flight above them. In a hideous voice the being screamed loudly,

"You will all die!"

After the Evil Being flew off, William looked back at the man in the rut and started asking more questions.

"Why did Deceit want us to leave you alone?" asked William.

"I do not know. You are no threat. Nobody can get me out of this rut. So, why did Addictions send one of his Dark Beings to scare you off?" asked the man in the rut.

Zom had just gotten done talking to Jeremiah and found out that Jeremiah had the power to free the man in the rut.

"I know why Deceit was trying to scare us off. It is because she knew that Jeremiah could undue King Addictions work and free the man in the rut!" exclaimed Zom.

"Is it true? Can you free me?" asked the man in the rut.

"seY, " said Jeremiah.

Jeremiah went up to William and started whispering in his ear. When Jeremiah was done, William looked at the man in the rut and said,

"If you want freedom from the rut you must think positive and believe that you can be free from the rut," said William.

The man in the rut cleared his mind and started thinking to himself, "I can be free...I can be free...I can be free."

After thinking this to himself over and over, the man in the rut started believing it. As a result of the man in the rut believing, he could be free the ground around him loosened, and he crawled out of the rut. When the man was free from the rut he vowed his help to the comrades.

"I am in your debt. Allow me to help you in any way that I can!" exclaimed the man.

"We are traveling to the castle of Addictions to do battle with him," William told the man.

"I have lost my soul and now my mind, so I will join you, for I have nothing to lose. Let us all go together and battle King Addictions," said the man from the rut

So it came to be, that our comrades took on another traveler. There was still some daylight left after the man in the rut was freed and the comrades continued their journey.

While on the journey, William asked the man from the rut his name. The man told William that his name was James and that he was born in the Village of Honesty. The man explained that he came to the Dark Side of the land to find a friend of his who was tall, but also very thin, with long lanky arms, big droopy-looking, green eyes and a very large nose.

Meanwhile, the Positive and Negative forces were gathering their armies for the battle. The Dark Knight, Insanity had gathered the most hideous Dark Beings possible for the battle. The Dark Forces were already arriving at the battleground. Up to now, our comrades have had a journey without many problems however, the closer they get to the dark castle the more difficult the journey will become!

CHAPTER TWENTY-TWO

DANIELLE'S TRIAL

In a damp and dimly lit room, in a lower part of King Addictions castle, a mock trial was just beginning. A large wooden podium sat in the middle of this particular room, and on the podium of this room stood Danielle, and she was very scared!

Around the podium were wooden benches and directly in front of the podium were a very large desk a chair to match. In the chair sat King Addictions. He was the judge.

The room became very noisy with all the Negative Beings talking among them about what punishment should be given to Danielle.Addictions had his face covered. Addictions face was so hideous that, if a human saw it, they would die of fright!

King Addictions looked out onto the crowd of other Dark Beings and roared. Then he spoke,

"Silence you fools, silence!"

The crowd of Dark Beings became very quiet. Then Addictions turned towards Danielle.

"You have been put on trial for crimes against the Dark Forces of

Negativity. How do you plead, guilty or not guilty?" shouted Addictions.

"I am guilty of nothing!" Danielle shouted out into the crowd.

"Silence, you Pathetic human! Silence, before I lift off my mask and show you horrors never before dreamed of in humanity!" shouted Addictions.

Addictions faced the crowd of Evil Beings and began to read the charges against Danielle. The crowd of Evil Beings was very quiet as King Addictions took out the scroll and opened it.

"The first charge against this pathetic human is refusing to give in to the negative peer pressure. The second charge is refusing to allow Alcohol and Drugs to enter into her life and last, but not least, attempting to help other people stay away from Alcohol and Drugs!" shouted Addictions.

Sneers and shouts began coming from the crowd of Dark Beings. Then, Sir Hate stood up and shouted,

"Guilty, guilty. The human is guilty!"

Hate began to get the rest of the crowd excited. Before long the whole crowd was pointing at Danielle and shouting,

"Condemn the human. Cast her into the pit!"

"She has committed a crime against the whole negative race!" shouted Ignorance.

Many other beings stood up to condemn Danielle. Among them were Envy, Want, and Disease. Hate was one of the worst of the Dark Beings because it could take on so many forms and show up in so many ways!

The courtroom was now getting very noisy and King Addictions was becoming impatient.

"Silence!" shouted Addictions.

Then the entire crowd of Dark Beings became silent. Addictions faced Danielle and shouted in a hideous voice,

"The court finds you guilty of all of the charges. What have you to say for yourself?"

Danielle answered,

"I try to follow the side of Positivity on a daily basis, because it makes life a good thing to have, instead of being a curse," answered Danielle.

Just then, another Dark Being stood up and began to speak. The being was Sir Prejudice.

'This human and her friends do not look like us, act like us or believe what we believe. They are animals and should be destroyed before more animals like they try to take over our land!" spoke Prejudice.

"Good point!" said Hate.

"Silence!" shouted Addictions.

"We treasure life. Is that a crime?" asked Danielle.

After Danielle told the Dark Beings that she treasured life, they all began laughing loudly,

"Life is pain, misery and death, you pathetic human. How can you say that happiness can be found among things such as these?" shouted Addictions.

"Happiness and good things can be found in anything, if they are sought for long enough," said Danielle.

"Your way is a hard road that involves much work and patience," said Addictions

"Happiness comes fast my way," he continued, growing more annoyed.

"Your way is fast, indeed, and your happiness is false and short-lived and requires a payment of life and soul!" exclaimed Danielle.

"Enough!" shouted Addictions.

The crowd of Dark Beings began shouting, "Guilty, the girl is guilty!"

"You have been found guilty of all charges and are sentenced to a fate worse than death!" shouted Addictions.

King Addictions ordered that Danielle's soul to be cast into the dungeons below the castle and that her body should be kept in the castle to rot!

"Shall I take her now, Dark Master?" asked Insanity.

"Yes. Take her below and separate her soul from her body. Then cast her soul in the dungeon and let her body rot!" commanded Addictions.

Insanity worked fast for he had an army to take into battle in a short time and had to get back to his soldiers.

Danielle's soul was locked in the dungeons, and her body was taken to the darkest part of the castle to rot. Meanwhile, the people who lived where the light still existed in nowhere land were in despair. The rumors on the streets were very bad. The rumors said that all was lost and that Addictions had won. And soon there would be no place in the land that did not belong to Negativity.

Back at the Castle of Negativity, sounds of laughter rang from the dark endless hole in the lower reaches of the castle.

Humankind will soon be mine, and all of their souls will become one with me!" exclaimed Negativity.

"Yes. Soon there will be no light in the Land of Nowhere at all," bragged King Addictions.

Truly, the situation was looking bad for the good people of nowhere land. Now they had come face to face with their Dark Side. The kingdom at this point was still divided into two sides, the Light and the Dark. Opposite as they were, both sides were still nowhere land. Would the Dark and Light continue to be, or would the darkness take over and cast the entire land into darkness?

Meanwhile, in the dungeon of the Dark King's castle, Danielle's soul drifted aimlessly with all of the other lost souls. One of the drifting souls approached Danielle's soul and asked,

"When will this nightmare end?"

"It will end for us when Negativity envelops our souls with eternal darkness, but we will be free before that happens," answered Danielle, still holding on to hope.

"I always believed that I would die only once," said the lost soul to Danielle.

"Addictions cause a person to be the living dead. People walk around acting like they are happy with life, but inside they are dead emotionally," answered Danielle.

"Is there no hope for me?" asked the lost soul who was in total misery.

"There is always hope. No matter how dark life gets, there is always hope hiding in the distance waiting to make its self known," answered Danielle.

Back at the hospital, Aggie whispered in Danny's ear,

"Listen, my sleeping friend. Without physical life, what good is emotional life, and why is it that good goals are so hard to reach?'

Danny stirred in his hospital bed, as if to answer the questions that Aggie had asked him.

"I see that you are listening to me, Danny.Now, listen well. Many things in life are easy to find, but they are just as easily lost. If we do not work to receive something, then we will not appreciate it as much. When we work hard for something, we are protective of it and work hard not to lose it," said Aggie.

Aggie knew in her heart that Danny heard and understood what she had said.

"Now, my sleeping friend, lets get back to nowhere land!" continued Aggie.

Well, things were looking dark for the Land of Nowhere. Danielle's soul was locked in the dungeons of the dark castle. William and his comrades were still on the side of the mountain traveling up to the dark castle, and the armies of Light and Dark were lined up on the castle grounds. It was a sight to see. Two armies, both not of this world, were going into battle.

Positivity had taken the form of a Knight in shining armor, and he carried a flag that had on it the symbol of eternal light. The symbol was a fiery torch with two swords on each side of the torch. All of the Positive Beings were mounted on horses and armed with their own weapons.

On the other side of the field, Insanity rode on the back of a dark horse. The dark horse had fiery red eyes and green skin but it appeared as black as death. All of the Dark Forces were behind Insanity awaiting orders to attack. If Hell exists, it certainly was sitting behind the dark horse of Insanity waiting to go into battle.

CHAPTER TWENTY-THREE

WILLIAM AND HIS FRIENDS APPROACH THE CASTLE OF ADDICTIONS

Meanwhile, William and his comrades was only a couple of miles from the castle of King Addictions and could see the castle from a distance.

"There it is. The castle of Addictions," exclaimed Vola.

"Yes. And it looks like a battle is about to start, but I have never seen beings like the ones getting ready to do battle," said William.

"We need to find the back of the castle. If we get caught up in that battle, we will not survive long enough to save Danielle and do battle with King Addictions," said Zom.

The five friends kept on the path to the castle, and when they were almost to the top, they got off of the path they were on and went into the woods behind the castle. When they reach the back of the castle they looked around the entire area to see if any Dark Beings were standing guard to the back door of the castle.

"I do not see any guards," said William.

"We should still play it safe and find another way into the castle," replied

Vola.

"Eh si thgri stel esu eht evac ecnartne tath seof ot eht noegnud!" exclaimed Jeremiah.

Jeremiah was pointing to a stream that appeared to be going into the castle.It was downhill from where our comrades were standing.

"Jeremiah says we should use the cave entrance to the dungeons, so we can get into the castle."

William looked in the direction that Jeremiah was pointing, and he saw the stream leading to the cave.

"Let's go. We have to get into the castle and find Danielle!" exclaimed William, who was becoming more and more hopeful that he would soon find her.

So our five comrades headed down the hill, following the stream into the cave, heading for the inside of the castle.

Everyone in the Land of Nowhere knew something was wrong because the ground was shaking and the skies turned very dark. All of the people of nowhere land hid in their houses and tried not to listen to the unearthly noises coming from the Dark Side of the land. The noises were coming from the battlefield outside of the castle of Addictions. The battle had begun, and it was a battle between two armies not of this world. On the battlefield the Good and Evil Beings were clashing and fighting.Insanity was fighting with Sanity. Happiness was fighting with Sadness. Fear was fighting with Courage. And Life was fighting with Death. There were arrows flying, swords clashing and beings falling from the sky wounded or dead. It was a sight to see!Many other beings were fighting on the battlefield, but they were too many to count!Night was fighting with Day, and Disease was fighting with Health. The battlefield was crowded with beings from another realm fighting to the death!

In the meantime, our five comrades were well on their way into the cave. It was very dark in the tunnel, and Vola lit one of the torches he had used in the cave leading out of the Land of the Deep.

Inside the castle, King Addictions was watching the battle from an upper room in the castle. After watching the battle for a while, Addictions decided to go to the lower level of the castle and speak with the Ancient Master, Negativity. Little did he know, that he was heading for the very place William and his friends were going!

On the battlefield, the battle raged on, just like the battles we face in our lives every day. At this time, the being, Hate, was guarding the dungeons. It would be Hate guarding the lost souls in the dungeon while Insanity was doing battle with his armies.Fear was on the battlefield but would leave the battle in an instant, if called upon by King Addictions.

Danielle's soul still wondered aimlessly in the dungeons of lost souls. Danielle was very strong, and she knew that the being, Hope, was near and would not let her end her life this way! While in the dungeon, she did not cry or give up the fight.Instead, she talked to other lost souls and gave them hope that someday they would be free!In the darkest times, the light is near. The dark times seem huge and never-ending, but they never dim the light of Hope.

In the tunnel, the five comrades came upon a great light and the entire tunnel was lit up! Within the light was the face of a young girl.Her eyes were ablaze with a brighter light!She looked at the five comrades and smiled. Then she walked towards William and his friends. She walked up next to them and stood there and looked them over. Then she spoke,

"I am Hope, the light that never dies, and I have been around since the time of existence itself. I know of your journey and am here to help you."

William and his friends could only look upon Hope for small periods of time, because of the brightness of her being.

"We are here seeking to find our friend Danielle and destroy Addictions," said William, covering his eyes from the light.

"You are truly brave my friends, but without help, you will be destroyed!" said Hope, still smiling.

"Then what can we do to destroy Addictions?" asked Zom.

"All of you must draw near to me, and stand in the warmth of my light," said Hope.

All five of the travelers gathered around Hope. Then Hope looked at the man from the rut and asked him if he believed in Hope. Upon hearing this, the man from the rut told her of his rescue and assured her that he did believe in Hope.

"Now that you are all in the warmth of my light, think only good thoughts," said Hope.

All of the comrades began to think good thoughts.Before long, all five of the comrades were transformed into light. The light disappeared from the cave. When the light re-appeared, the five comrades were in a different land! William and his friends opened their eyes and looked around.

"We are not in the cave anymore. Where are we?" asked William, speechless from the beauty of the land he now found himself in.

"Indeed, you are not in the cave. Now you are in the Land Of The Good!" exclaimed Hope

CHAPTER TWENTY-FOUR

WILLIAM BATTLES FEAR

After being told that they were in the Land Of The Good, our five comrades began looking around. What they saw was amazing to them. In front of them was a mountain made of clear crystal. Sitting on top of the mountain was a castle made of silver. The land they were in was covered with blue lakes and snow topped mountains.

In the sky around the castle were what appeared to be angels flying in and out of the castle? The angels were surrounded by light and all of them were happy and content.

"This is the Land Of The Good, where I am to seek the help of the Wizard!" exclaimed William.

Just then, a thunderous voice came from all directions in the Land Of The Good.

"William, I see you made it to my land with all of you're friends. There is much I have to tell you before you go back to the realm from where you came," spoke the voice of the Wizard.

"Can you show yourself to us?" asked Zom.

"You have seen me before, when I answered your summons. Everything you see around you in your life that makes you feel good - is me. I am in you and all around you.I am life," said the Wizard.

"What are you?" asked Vola.

"Some call me God. Others call me a Wizard, yet others, call me Nature. What I am called means little. The fact is, that I exist," answered the Wizard.

"Why do you allow Addictions to destroy nowhere land?" asked Zom.

"I do not allow it. The Dark Side has been around as long as I have, and they will always try to make life dark. It is their nature. Without Bad, what meaning would Good have?" answered the Wizard.

"How can we destroy King Addictions?" asked William.

"King Addictions cannot be destroyed, but he can be stopped from causing much of the damage that he causes," spoke the Wizard.

"You mean, he can be slowed down and nothing else?" asked William, getting very frustrated at this point.

"At the present time, he can be slowed down, but if you do as I tell you, there may be a day when King Addictions can be destroyed and cast back into Eternal Darkness," replied the Wizard.

"I will do as you tell me," said William.

"I will not speak to you about it in front of any other being, therefore, I will imprint it on your mind, and when the time comes, you will already know what to do." said the wizard, known by some as God.

After the wizard told William what had to be said, the wizard's voice was quiet. All of the comrades were wondering what was to happen next.

"I sense that Danielle's soul has been taken from her body and cast into the dungeons of Addiction's castle. Even now, she calls for me," spoke Hope.

"We must get to the castle and free Danielle!" exclaimed William.

"Be prepared for an attack by one of Addictions' Dark Knights. This, I can sense, is coming soon," said Hope.

Once again, the Light of Hope took on a stronger form, and the comrades were brought back to the castle of King Addictions.

King Addictions was well on his way to the dungeons when the castle started to shake under him, and a voice came out of the pit in the bottom of the castle.

"King Addictions...it is I, Negativity,"

King Addictions fell to his knees and trembled.

"Yes, oh ancient Dark One, I hear you. What is it you want of me?" asked Additions, in a fearful voice.

"You have visitors in the castle, and they have entered through the cave behind the castle and are traveling to the dungeons to free their pathetic friend, Danielle," answered Negativity.

"I will surely destroy them, oh, Dark One!" exclaimed Additions.

"Listen to me, you idiot. They have just come back from the Realm of the Good where they have been speaking with my father. Be cautious, Addictions. My father fights for the wrong side, but he is no fool," said Negativity.

"As you say, Ancient Master. I will be cautious," replied Addictions.

After speaking with Negativity, Addictions decided to call Fear off the battlefield to destroy William and his friends.

Fear was on the battlefield fighting with Courage when he heard the Dark King call for him.

"Come, Fear. Come now to my side and help me to destroy the boy William and his companions who were sent here to destroy me."

Addictions said with his mind.

On the battlefield Fear knew that he had to obey King Addictions, but he was angry about not finishing his fight with Courage.

"You have escaped my wrath this time Courage, but we will meet again soon, and I will destroy you!" shouted Fear.

After his threats to Courage, Fear left the battlefield and headed for the dark castle of Addictions.

Meanwhile, William and his friends were back in the cave heading for the dungeons. The Light of Hope was leading them on.

Fear was told by King Addictions to guard the dungeons doors and to destroy William and his friends when they arrived to free Danielle.

William and his friends finally arrived at the dungeons of the lost souls, and they all began looking around the chamber.

"I cannot believe that an evil gatekeeper is not guarding the door to the dungeons of lost souls," said Vola, in a fearful voice.

"Zom. Go and find Danielle's body and protect it with your life!" William said in a pleading voice.

"Do not worry my friend. I will find Danielle and protect her until her soul is back inside her body," said Zom.

Zom looked around to ask Hope what to do next, but she was gone.

"How will we open the dungeons door when it is locked up tight?" asked Vola.

"We will have to break the lock," said William, looking very determined.

Vola spotted a torch holder on the wall that was made of metal.

"We must take the torch holder off the wall and smash the lock off of the dungeons door!" exclaimed Vola.

As Vola was speaking, a dark mist entered the chamber by way of the stairway leading to the main floor of the castle. Before anyone noticed, it had completely surrounded William.

William suddenly became very fearful, and his heart was beating fast, and he felt an overwhelming fear that seemed to coming out of nowhere.

Then a voice echoed in the castle chamber, "See how easily I capture this human. He is pathetic, I will play with his mind for awhile and then destroy him," spoke the hideous voice of Fear.

William was frozen with Fear, and could not move.

"You are next creature from the deep, and then I will destroy the other human and the backwards boy!" exclaimed Fear.

Now the mist that was Fear took on the appearance of a robed and hooded man of about seven feet tall. The eyes of the man glowed red. Vola saw what was happening to William and made a mad rush at the hooded figure, trying to stop it from hurting William.

Fear grew lanky green fingernails and pointed one of his fingers at Vola. A flash, of what appeared to be fire, came from the hooded figure's finger and struck Vola, knocking the creature of the deep ten feet in the air and up against a brick wall of the chamber. Vola was now unconscious.

"You stupid, sad creature. You cannot destroy me. I am immortal!" exclaimed Fear.

Jeremiah who was standing with his back toward Fear, looked in the opposite direction and said,

"esucxE em rm. raeF, dluoc uoy esaelp pots gnitruh ym s'dneirf?"

"What did that backward freak just say too me?" asked Fear, in an angry voice.

"As near as I can figure, he asked you to stop hurting his friend," said the man from the rut.

Upon hearing this, Fear became very angry. He pointed his finger at Jeremiah and shot fire at him. Well, of course, with Jeremiah being who he was, the fire reversed itself and hit Fear in the chest, knocking him backwards.

"It is times like these, I think it would be much safer being back in my rut!" exclaimed the man from the rut.

After picking himself up off the ground, Fear looked at Jeremiah and thought,

"What kind of being is this?"

"That was very witty of you, but now you die, you backwards freak!" shouted Fear in an angry voice.

Just as Fear was getting ready to send the most powerful burst of fire he could summons to destroy Jeremiah, the castle began to shake, and a loud voice came from thin air, "Fear, you have brought about your own end by trying to destroy Jeremiah. Everything you try to do will reverse itself, and now you have brought me here to help Jeremiah destroy you!" exclaimed Truth

Fear began to laugh loudly, and when he was done laughing, he replied,

"You are wrong, Truth. You are the one who will be destroyed!" shouted

Fear in a mocking voice.

At that point, Fear shot very powerful fireballs out of his fingers towards Truth.

Only another Being from a higher realm could see Truth because, at this moment, Truth was in its purest form. The fireballs hit Truth knocking the Being of Light up against the chambers north wall. After brushing off the effect of the fireballs, Truth took the form of a white dragon and flew towards Fear. The dragon was quick to come down on Fear and knocked him to the ground.

Fear got back up and continued shooting fire from his fingers.

The battle was fierce. The dragon had a large wingspan and fiery breath. Its eyes were a deep blue and the entire body of it was white. Both of the beings continued to fight Jeremiah and the man from the rut hid behind the staircase to avoid being destroyed.

William, who was now freed from the mist of Fear, remembered something the Wizard had planted in his mind. William began looking around the chamber. When he could not find what he needed, he went into one of the hallways that led out from the chamber. William entered a sleeping chamber.

In the sleeping room, William found a goblet and a silver plate that were used for eating and drinking. Both the goblet and the plate were made of silver and were shiny. Upon seeing this, William picked up the silver plate and began polishing it up with his shirt. The entire time William was shining the plate, he was remembering one of the things the wizard had implanted in his mind. The Wizard had told William that the being, Fear, could not stand to see its own reflection. If Fear saw his reflection, he would turn on himself and be sent to the bottomless pit of Negativity for a period of time before he could once again be released to the Land of Nowhere.

William finished polishing the plate and went back out into the chamber where Truth and Fear were doing battle. When William walked into the chamber, he caught the attention of Fear. When Fear saw William, he grabbed hold of the dragon and threw it across the chamber and spoke,

"You...You are the one who has come to destroy King Addictions. I will kill you first. Then I will deal with Truth!" exclaimed Fear.

Fear walked up to William, grabbed hold of his shirt and picked him up off the ground.

"Now you will die pathetic human!" shouted Fear.

Holding William up in the air, Fear was going to cut the human in half with one of his fingernails. William brought the silver plate out in front of his body and Fear saw the plate.

"Look everybody. The human has brought a plate to destroy me with!" mocked Fear.

Fear began laughing at William, and the laugh was so loud that it echoed throughout the Land of Nowhere on the Light and Dark Sides of the land.

As Fear laughed birds fell dead from the sky and trees wilted and died. The rot of death was in the air!

"A plate will not help you, boy," said Fear.

"Fear was just getting ready to kill William, when he saw his own reflection in the plate. The Dark Being began to scream in agony. Then he dropped William on the floor and put his hands to his face.

"I have been tricked by the human boy!" screamed Fear in a hideous voice.

Just then a huge set of hands came up from the floor of the castle and laid hold of Fear.

"No, Ancient Master. King Addictions has need of my services. Do not take me back to the pit of hell!" screamed Fear in terror.

No matter how hard the Dark Being, Fear, fought, he could not stop the hands from dragging him down through the floor and into the pit.

Jeremiah and the man from the rut stood and watched, in disbelief, as Fear disappeared into the floor and was gone. Truth had left the form of the white dragon and, once again, was not visible.

William went over to Vola and picked him up off the floor. Vola was shaken up and badly bruised but still alive. Jeremiah and the man in the rut joined back up with William and Vola. William took the torch holder off the wall and smashed the lock off the dungeons door.

CHAPTER TWENTY-FIVE

ZOM MEETS IGNORANCE

In the meantime, Zom had found the body of Danielle and was staying close to it in order to protect her. As Zom was standing next to Danielle's body, he heard a clumping sound on the floor in the next chamber. It sounded like several clumps at a time only not all at the same time.

Zom became curious about the sound so he walked over to the next chamber room and looked inside. What he saw filled him with terror.

In the next room and coming towards the chamber Zom was in, there was a huge black spider! It had long lanky legs. The spider had eight legs and a huge oval shaped body. It also had huge green eyes and large fangs filled with poison.

Zom knew the spider was coming for Danielle and himself. Zom was willing to fight to the death to protect his friend.

Back at the chamber where the dungeons of the lost souls were, William and the man from the rut smashed the lock to the dungeon door and swung the door open wide. All at once, thousands of lost souls came flooding out of the dungeons!

King Addictions had just walked into the chamber at the same time the souls were fleeing the dungeons. The chamber was lit up with the light of all the souls escaping. Some of the souls had bodies to go back to. However, the souls that had no bodies, had passed on into the Land Of The Good. Some of the souls recognized King Addictions and began attacking him! Addictions fled to an upper part of the castle to avoid being overwhelmed by the lost souls. Danielle's soul fled the dungeons and went looking for its body.

Back at the chamber where Zom and Danielle's body were, the spider had now entered, while Zom stood guarding Danielle's body.

With all of its eight legs moving at different times, the spider made its way up to where Zom was standing and stopped. Much to the surprise of Zom, the spider began to talk!

"You are Zom, a creature of the deep. Why do you protect the human?" asked the spider.

"We protect the humans because we are a lot like they are," replied Zom.

"The humans would never protect you," said the spider in a sly way.

"Humans have protected us in the past," answered Zom.

"Humans think that they are superior to you, and they lead you around by the nose and use you when it is in their best interest," replied the spider.

"That is not true," said Zom, becoming angry at the spider.

"It is true. Life is a sick joke. One needs to use everybody one can and get rid of them when they are of no use anymore," said the spider, in a sly way.

"I do not believe that," answered Zom.

"It matters little what you believe. My fangs carry a very deadly poison and the poison is called Ignorance. Once bitten, you will see the truth in Ignorance," said the spider, trying to sound convincing.

The spider began to get closer to Zom, and it was just getting ready to bite him when, a bright light flew into the chamber and attacked the spider. The spider took action against the light. It moved around the chamber with lightening speed trying to kill the light. The light circled the spider three times and flew directly into the body of the spider! The spider came to a standstill. Holes appeared on the body of the spider and light was shining out of the holes.

The spider began making a high-pitched screaming sound, and its whole body started to shake. Zom saw that the spider was about to explode, so he jumped on top of Danielle's body to protect it. After shaking for a few moments the spider's body exploded! The spider's body parts flew all over the chamber, and the spider was no more.

When things calmed down a bit, Zom got up and began cleaning parts of the spider's body off of himself. The light that entered the body of the spider appeared again, and Zom did not know what to think of it. The light became brighter, and it flew right past Zom and into the body of Danielle. After a few seconds Danielle opened her eyes and saw Zom.

"Zom, is that you?" asked Danielle.

"Yes, it is me, and thank the Land Of The Good that you are back in your body!" exclaimed Zom.

"I feel as though I have just awakened from a nightmare!" exclaimed Danielle, still feeling groggy.

"You must get up. We still need to confront King Addictions," said Zom.

William and his friends were in the hallways looking for Zom. Danielle and Zom were looking for William and the others. King Addictions was now on the upper level of the castle speaking to Negativity.

"Oh, Ancient Master, the human and his comrades have cast Fear into the dark pit and cast Ignorance out of the castle, and, now, they have come for me!" exclaimed Addictions in a pleading voice.

"I have called Insanity in from the battlefield to speak the incantation that will open up the gates to the bottomless pit, so the creatures of Hell can roam the earth for a short time," replied Negativity.

"Thank you, Ancient One. With the help of the inhabitants of the pit, I will surely defeat the human and his friends," spoke Addictions, feeling more confident now.

Back down in the lower reaches of the castle, William and his friends met up with Danielle and Zom. William ran to Danielle and held her in his arms.

"You are back.I have missed you so much and have worried about you, my friend!" exclaimed William, as relief swept over his face.

"I have been in a nightmare that seemed like it lasted forever," replied Danielle.

"What happened to you after you were taken from the ship?" asked William.

"The Dark Ones put me on trial and found me guilty. Then they put my soul in the dungeons of lost souls," said Danielle happy to be back with her friends.

"We are all happy to see you Danielle, but we have to find Addictions and destroy him while there is still time!" exclaimed Vola.

After their reunion, our group of battle weary warriors headed for the stairs leading to the main part of the Dark Castle. For a while, nobody spoke, but they all knew that Danielle was truly a brave and strong human and that her tale of victory against Ignorance would be told for ages to come!

Unknown to William and his friends, the Dark Knight, Insanity, was coming from the battlefield at that very moment to speak the incantation that would open up the gates of the bottomless pit.

CHAPTER TWENTY-SIX

THE BATTLE WITH ADDICTIONS

When storms rule the earth and Death is the king,
And the hands of the clock refuse to swing.

When the living is dead but still walking around,
And when nothing good can be said or be found.

Then comes a very sad, sad sight.
'Tis the death of a world that refuses to fight.

Weep human kind for your children and kin.
Weep human kind for the misery within.

When a world is all ravaged and bitter and worn,
Between all of the opposites a realm has been torn.

So it came to past that the incantation was spoken over the bottomless pit.
Insanity was speaking the incantation with a dark joy, knowing what it

would bring about.

William and his friends were still climbing the stairs to the main part of the castle when a lost soul blocked their path. The lost soul spoke to William's soul. The lost soul was that of King Nobody.

" I have heard of your courage, William., I was deceived by Deceit and by King Addictions, but, now that my soul is free, I will return to my worn body and do all in my power to battle Addictions!" spoke the soul of King Nobody in a very determined way.

Thus, King Nobody was on his way to being King Somebody.

Immediately after the incantation was spoken, every Dark Being known to eternity came out of the pit. Laughing and cackling the Dark Beings took flight. Knowing their time was short, the Dark Beings aimed at doing as much damage as possible to the Land of Nowhere. The Dark Beings flew North, South, East and West. All four corners of the earth were their targets. After they had brought destruction to the land, they would come back and destroy William and his friends, for surely it would not take long to destroy nowhere land.

Although the Dark Beings could not be seen with the human eye, they still did their damage to the world. Jealousy, Sorrow and Confusion, were among them.All of the other Dark Beings who were not on the battlefield were unleashed on the world. These Dark Beings were set free to bring Hell to earth.

William and Danielle, along with their friends, met King Addictions when they reached the main part of the castle. King Addictions was in his black robe and had his mask on, thankfully. On his shoulders were two weapons.One was Alcohol and the other Drugs.

"At last, we meet in person. I see that the girl has escaped the dungeons. No matter. Now, I shall kill all of you," spoke Addictions, in a sarcastic voice.

"You have hurt my people and ruined our land. Why do you destroy us?" asked Vola, in an angry voice.

"It is because you beings are so stupid. Look at yourselves. I destroy you by the thousands and still you do not believe that I exist!" exclaimed Addictions.

"You deceived my people and killed them and ruined everything around them. You are a coward!" shouted Vola.

At this point, the thing called Alcohol, which appeared as a poisonous spider, began to move down King Addictions' body heading towards Vola.

"Patience, Alcohol, and get back on my shoulder. I am not yet ready to kill them!" exclaimed Addictions.

The spider, with its long lanky legs, was brown and hair. It had huge fangs and was the size of a large cat. It went back up onto King Addictions' shoulder and stood still. On the other shoulder of Addictions was Drugs. It was in the form of a large scorpion and was red in color. It had a huge stinger on its tail.

"You speak very tough, indeed, for a half human and half fish!" exclaimed Addictions, with an evil grin on his face.

"You are the reason that our city and land was destroyed!" exclaimed Vola, angrily.

"Not true. Every being in that city had a choice, and they chose me," said Addictions.

"You sent your Dark Beings to make us weak, so you could take our souls," shouted Zom who was getting angrier by the minute.

"Wrong again. The Dark Beings have always been here. You chose to listen to them," replied Addictions, enjoying every minute.

"No matter what you say, the world will be better off without you," said Danielle.

Negativity had been listening to the talk between King Addictions and William's friends. Negativity decided to help King Addictions by stopping time, as we know it.

Once Negativity stopped time, Addictions could do whatever he wanted to with the bodies of the pathetic human boy and his friends.

The ancient Dark Master reached his hands into eternity and stopped time! At that very moment, William and his friends were frozen in time and unable to move. Addictions knew that his master had frozen time to help him destroy his enemies.

"Oh, thank you, my master, for you have made my job so much easier," spoke Addictions.

So, there stood King Addictions, who smelled of decay and had the darkest of souls, thinking what would be the best way to destroy the pathetic beings.

The Dark King thought maybe he would burn their bodies, or maybe he would feed them to one of his many pets. Better yet, he would hang them by the neck and put them on display in the other side of nowhere land, as an example to anyone who would seek to destroy him!

The Dark King looked at William and his friends and knew he had won. King Addictions began to laugh, and his laugh echoed off every corner of the earth, and the reek of decay was in every part of the Land of Nowhere.

In the meantime, Envy and Greed were destroying many beings in the Land of Nowhere. These two Dark Beings were causing humans to turn against humans. They were causing village to turn against village.

After Envy and Greed were done, they would let their dark brother,

Murder, take his pick of victims. The Land of Nowhere was without order. It was in chaos, and, once in chaos, the Dark Being, Poverty, began roaming the land. Beings were stealing from there fellows, and they were killing their own kind for money. Many people of nowhere land went into hiding to keep from getting robbed and killed.

The wizard in the Land Of The Good was very sad about what was happening to the Land of Nowhere but was unable to stop his son Negativity from his dark deeds. Suddenly, Negativity's voice rose from the pit and thundered in the Land of the Good.

"Father...father...it is I, your son, Negativity, and you are powerless to stop me so why not join me in destroying the pathetic Land of Nowhere?" asked Negativity, in a voice that kills all living things.

"You still do not see the truth my son, and it saddens me," replied the Wizard, as he stared down into the pit of darkness.

"The truth is, that nothing matters, and that the only thing that life can bring is death," spoke Negativity.

"Yes, my son, death will come to all beings who are not immortal like ourselves, but it matters greatly what the mortals do during one lifetime!" exclaimed the Wizard in a serious tone of voice.

"How can anything matter when death is the final reward?" asked Negativity.

"Without the belief that the humans have, we would not exist. They are a part of us, my son. But, you cannot see past your greed and your desire to be the master of all of existence," answered the Wizard.

"They are nothing but food for my world, father, and they are good for nothing else!" spoke Negativity in an angry voice.

"You are wrong my son, for the truth is, that each one of the mortals count and what one mortal does affects many other mortals, and that affects our Realm," spoke the Wizard, in a kind way.

"You are a blind fool father, and someday you will kneel down and kiss my feet!" spoke Negativity in a mocking voice.

With this, Negativity crawled deeper into the bottomless pit, and on his way down he chanted,

"Kill...kill...kill..

At this point the great white Wizard's eyes were on the events taking place in the castle of King Addictions.

The Wizard knew that mortal beings were born with the knowledge that a spiritual world existed. He knew that times would change and technology, along with science, would advance but that nothing would ever change the laws of the immortal beings.

Back at the castle of King Addictions, time, as we know it, had stopped.

King Addictions decided to call on Confusion to come into the castle and put William and his friends through some suffering before he had them hanged.

Confusion came to the castle of Addictions right away and took the form of a red mist. The red mist floated through a window in the upper castle and down to the main part of the castle. Then it floated right in front of King Addictions.

"What do you wish of me, oh, Dark King?" asked Confusion.

"Make a mist into a blanket and cover these pathetic beings in Confusion," commanded Addictions.

Knowing that the human and his friends had come to destroy Addictions, Confusion did as he was told and floated over to William and his friends, covering them in the red mist of Confusion.

The affect was fast and the mist put all of its victims in the constant state of misery, which was emotional confusion.

William and Danielle were now suffering in their souls. Zom and Vola, along with the man from the rut, were also suffering. Jeremiah, on the other hand, was feeling good and laughing. This angered Addictions.

"Why are you not frozen in time, and why do you laugh instead of suffer?" asked Addictions, now getting somewhat confused himself.

"I ma a drawkcab gnieb, rof meht, emit ezorf, rof em ti ezorf nu, daetsni, fo gnieb desufnoc, ym dnim si yrev raelc!" exclaimed Jeremiah.

Jeremiah told the Dark King that his spell had unfrozen him in time and that Confusion only made his mind clearer. The little child from the Village of Backwards was more powerful than the Dark King had thought!

King Addictions remembered the Village of Backwards from past dealing with the people of the village, but thought that he was more powerful than anyone in the village.

Addictions knew all of the languages of the land and understood what Jeremiah had just told him. The Dark King began jumping up and down to the point where the castle started to shake.

"Cursed be this stupid little backward child. I can defeat any enemy pitted against me, but cannot destroy this backwards little child!" shouted Additions.

Suddenly, Jeremiah started walking towards the red mist called Confusion.

"Be gone, child, for I have no dealings with you!" shouted Confusion.

Jeremiah did not listen. He just kept on walking backwards towards the red mist. Jeremiah walked right into the red mist.

"Be gone, boy!" shouted Confusion.

Jeremiah's backwards ways began to undo the Confusion and turn it into clear-mindedness. Confusion felt itself growing weak and fled from the castle against King Addictions' wishes.

Jeremiah began touching all of his friend's arms. Upon touching his friend's arms, they were all unfrozen from time and able to move again!

William immediately remembered the other thing that the Wizard had put in his mind. The wizard told him that, in order to do great damage to King Addictions, he must unmask the Dark King so that all the beings in the Land of Nowhere could see what was under his mask.

Suddenly, another lost soul's light entered the room that William and his friends were in and went directly to the man from the rut. The lost soul entered the man from the rut.

"It is a miracle. I have gotten my soul back!" shouted the man from the rut in a joyous voice.

The man from the rut now appeared to have real life back in his body, and he was looking at King Addictions in a way that said,

"This is your fault!"

"Now, the Dark King was really angry. The Dark King held his hands out in front of him and began to summons demons from everywhere to come and destroy William and his comrades! Before the Dark King could complete the summons, William rushed towards King Addictions and jumped on him!

King Addictions was very strong. He grabbed William and threw him up against his friends who broke his fall. However, before King Addictions threw William off, the human boy had unmasked the Dark King.

Addictions began to scream and put his hands up to his face to hide it.

At the same time that William had unmasked King Addictions; the wizard had reflected the Dark King's face in the skies above the Land of Nowhere.

Every being in the land had a look at the face that was beneath the mask of King Addictions!

The face of the Dark King was hideous. It was wrinkled and had scabs all over it. The Dark King's teeth were rotted out of his head, and his eyes were a putrid green. Underneath the mask of Addictions was another being, and this being is known as Disease!

Now, all the beings of nowhere land knew that they were dealing with a disease not just a Dark King, but a living, breathing disease!By having this new knowledge about King Addictions, they no longer feared the Dark King, but they did fear Disease that hid under the mask of Addictions.

"I have been unmasked!" the Dark King screamed in horror.

"Look. He...It is a Disease!" exclaimed Vola in a surprised voice.

"You have won the battle William, but you will lose the war. Most beings will never believe that I am a Disease. That would mean they would have to quit using the magic potions, and they will never do that!" shouted Addictions.

"Maybe. But now, all the beings of nowhere land will have the idea in their minds that maybe you are a disease. And they will find a way to be rid of you," said William.

Pus was coming out of the pores in the face of Disease. Then it looked towards the Heavens and shouted,

"You have not won, Wizard! Along with my Dark Knights, I will destroy good and bad alike. I will lay to waste beings of every race, creed and gender!"

Addictions was becoming even weaker as he shouted towards the heavens once again,

"I will destroy rich and poor alike. I will lay them all to waste and feed their immortal souls to Negativity!"

"King Addictions...King Addictions...It is time for you to return to the pit of Hell. There you will gain strength and once again be unleashed on a world which refuses to believe you exist!" spoke Negativity to the mind of Addictions.

At that point, the shell called Addictions, which carried Disease in it, began to slowly fade away a little at a time until the Dark King and his two pets were finally gone!

As King Addictions was fading away, all of the Dark Beings from the pit of Hell were also called back.

CHAPTER TWENTY-SEVEN

THE LAND OF NOWHERE
RETURNS TO THE LIGHT

At the very time that King Addictions vanished, the Land of Nowhere began to become bright and sunny again. Even part of the Dark Side of Nowhere land became clean and new again, but the land around the Dark King's castle stayed dark and ugly, as if awaiting the return of its King

The battle of the Light and Dark Beings fought on the battlefield outside the Dark King's castle had stopped, for the present, until the two armies had rested for a while.

The people and creatures of nowhere land felt hope for the first time in a long time. All of the people and creatures of the land started helping each other rebuild their lives. The skies were blue again, and the nights were cool and filled with diamond like stars.

After resting for a few days, William and Danielle and their friends began the journey back to their homes. For a while, our brave warriors walked together and talked among themselves.

"We have won!" shouted Vola.

"No. We have not won, but now we have a chance to defeat Addictions," answered William.

"Where do we go now?" asked Danielle.

"We go back to our homes," answered William.

"We must stay in touch!" exclaimed the man from the rut.

"We will stay in touch, all of us," answered Zom.

All of our friends, who so bravely faced King Addictions, began their journeys home.

When Jeremiah returned home, he was thought of as a hero, and many of his fellow villagers were waiting to greet him with a parade and much merriment.

The first thing that Jeremiah did when got home was to walk up to the old man in the village and tell him that he was right. Jeremiah told the old man that, truly, "What is done, can be undone!"

When Zom and Vola retuned home, the whole city was waiting to crown them heroes.All of the streets of the city were full of beings cheering and waving to Zom and Vola. It looked like maybe they could have a chance to live above ground once again!

William and Danielle traveled to the Village of Honesty, and, as time passed, they married and began a family.

All the of the beings in the land, which was now called Somewhere land, were helping each other get off and stay off of the magic potions.All of the people and creatures of the land had taken a stand against Addictions. Knowing that Addictions was a Disease, the inhabitants of somewhere land created tools to fight against the Disease that was Addictions.

Immediately after William and his friends left the castle on their journeys back home, Negativity declared that the war on Positivity would go on for eternity! The war would shake the very foundation of existence! Who will win this war? We shall see in the next chapter!

DANNY'S SOUL RETURNS TO HIS BODY.

After seeing the final act of the battle against King Addictions, Danny felt his soul take flight. Once again, his soul was on the move. This time Danny's soul was not going down. It was going up! As his soul continued to travel upward Danny remembered everything that he had seen.Danny felt as though he had a new view on Addictions, and he never wanted to touch drugs or alcohol again, that is, if he even had another chance at life.

While Danny's soul was traveling upward, he heard another loud thunderous voice,

"You will live...You will live...You will live."

Suddenly, Danny's soul was back in his body, but his future was still in question. Still hooked up to life support and in a coma state, Danny could only hope that the powers that be would have mercy on him!

CHAPTER TWENTY-EIGHT

POSITIVITY BATTLES NEGATIVITY

Well. King Addictions was gone. As a result of the Dark King vanishing, all of the Evil Beings released on the world were called back to the dark pit where Negativity dwelt. Back at the Dark Castle, the Ancient Master, Negativity, was angry and ready to fight! Out of the dark pit in the castle where Addictions once lived, came a loud and thunderous voice that the whole land could hear, "Hear me Positivity, my brother. I am coming for you and will destroy you, once and for all."

When Negativity spoke, the force of his voice leveled trees and mountains! All of the people of nowhere land were in fear. They knew that a battle was coming between two powerful forces.

In the other realms of existence, all of the beings felt the anger of Negativity. All beings looked toward the sky, because they knew that was where the battle would be fought! At the time Negativity was shouting his anger, Positivity was in the Land Of The Good with his father, the wizard.

"Your brother calls on you to do battle with him," said the Wizard, sometimes called God.

"I am prepared to do battle, Father, but he must come for me first!" exclaimed Positivity.

The battle was starting, and all the Negative Beings were putting on their battle armor. Likewise, all of the Positive Beings were preparing for another battle with the Negative Beings. The sign of the beginning of the battle was the blowing of a horn that would sound in nowhere land and all of the other realms of existence.

The horn blower was Death, and when the horn blew, it was loud and thunderous. All of existence knew that it was the start of the battle between the Light and the Dark.

The Negative Beings flew from the bottomless pit and headed for the skies above nowhere land. Their leader, Negativity, was on a blood red chariot and had the Sword of Darkness with him. The sword that Negativity carried was known to destroy entire worlds with one blow.

Pulling Negativity's chariot were some of his favorite Dark Beings. Terror was one of them. Another was Misery, and two others were War and Poverty. The Dark Beings pulling the chariot for Negativity took the form of horses. The horse, Terror, was pale blue. The horse, Misery, was sickly yellow.

The two other horses were War, which was blood red, and Poverty, which was pale green.

"Ride hard, my dark comrades. For now is the time to destroy my ancient brother, Positivity, forever!" shouted Negativity.

Negativity began cracking his whip on the horses and flying his chariot towards the sky. When the ancient Dark Master had arrived at a certain place in the sky, he stopped the chariot and told his army to wait until he gave the order to attack.

All of the Positive Beings were waiting in the Village of Hope for the order from Positivity to do battle.

Negativity appears to people in different forms. However, at this time, he used the form of a giant half wolf and half man. The upper half of the ancient Dark Master was wolf. The lower half was man. In the chariot with Negativity was King Addictions along with his friends Alcohol and Drugs.

All of the inhabitants of nowhere land could look to the sky and see the Ancient Master, Negativity, on his chariot laughing hideously. When Negativity laughed, lightening bolts shot from his fingers and lit up all of the skies in existence. After the laughter Negativity began to shout.

"Curse you, Positivity, and curse all that is good!"

King Addictions looked at Negativity and asked.

"How many souls shall I steal? How many lives shall I destroy, oh Ancient Master?"

"Take all. Destroy all. Kill all. Kill...kill...kill." Negativity answered.

After waiting a while, Negativity saw that there were no Positive Beings to fight on the battlefield.

"My Brother, where are you and your army? Are you all cowards?" shouted Negativity. The anger of Negativity shook the very foundation of nowhere land.It caused the dead to rise and walk the land in confusion. It darkened the whole of the land but only for a little while.

Negativity was tired of waiting, so he reached up to the sky and, with his wolf's claws, tore a rip in the Land Of The Good, which blinded him for a short time.

Behind the rip stood Positivity. When the rip in the Land Of The Good took place, a bright light radiated from it, and all of the realms were lit up with a brilliant, white light.

Negativity put his head down, because he hated the light. Looking up into the sky, all of the beings beheld Positivity with his long white hair and beard. Positivity appeared to be pure white. The form of Positivity was draped with a white robe. In the Being of Light's right hand was a staff, and in his left hand was an hourglass.Looking into the hourglass, Positivity spoke,

"These are the sands of time, and I am the Keeper of Time. I am the voice heard by many and followed by some," spoke Positivity.

Positivity called upon his Positive Beings to leave the Village of Hope and come to stand by his side. When they joined Positivity, one of the Positive Beings stood on his right side. That Being was Honesty. The other being stood on the left side of Positivity. That being was Hope.

Negativity beheld his ancient brother, and spoke,

"We meet again my Brother!"

"It is true. Once again we meet, my Dark Brother," answered Positivity.

"Why do you continue to fight against me?" asked Negativity.

"You know why. That is just the way it is." answered Positivity.

"If you stand by my side, we will rule all of eternity!" exclaimed Negativity.

"If I stand by your side, we will be the rulers of Hell." answered Positivity.

"Why can't we rule eternity as brothers?" asked Negativity.

"It is not possible. In order to keep the balance of eternity, we must forever oppose each other," answered Positivity.

"It is sad that you will not join me. Now, the only thing I can do is destroy you," spoke Negativity.

No sooner than he had finished speaking to Positivity, Negativity ordered his army to attack.

Arrows were flying and swords were clashing, but no sooner then one Dark or Light Being was killed, they come back to life and continue fighting.

Stars were falling from the sky, and lightening was lighting up the sky. The whole of nature was at war! For a while, the war was continuous, but after a while it slowed down. There would be battles and retreats. As time went on, the retreats became longer. During these times the sun would shine, the flowers would grow and peace would return to the Land of Nowhere. All the worlds of eternity were becoming balanced again.

King Nobody was getting help to stay away from Addictions and was now becoming known as King Somebody.

All of Nowhere land was taking interest in their fellow mortals' feelings, and as a result, the entire land was becoming more united. Everyone in the land was helping each other fight against King Addictions, and Honesty was becoming a regular visitor to Nowhere land, which, by the way, was now being called Somewhere land.

"Who will have the final victory in the war between Positivity and Negativity? Will the Ancient Master, Negativity, end up being the ruler of all eternity? That, my sleeping friend is a good question!" exclaimed Aggie, talking to Danny at the hospital.

"Now, to end our journey," said Aggie.

Negativity, as well as Positivity, will always exist and so will all of the Negative and Positive Beings. They live in every thread and fiber of existence. Who will we choose to follow? As the battle against Addictions rages on, many people will die and many others will be scarred for life.

It has been said that every star that shines brightly in the night sky is the light of Positivity and every bit of darkness around the stars is Negativity.

On a stormy night, when the wind is whipping furiously about and when lightening is lighting up the sky and the sound of thunder is shaking the earth, then, cast your eyes toward the sky and know in your hearts that, once again, Positivity and Negativity are doing battle.

EPILOGUE

A ggie took her hand from Danny's and whispered in his ear, "You know the truth now, Danny. You have been set free, if you choose to be, and when you awaken and are able to leave this place, tell all the other people who suffer under King Addictions what you have seen in Nowhere land."

Aggie stood up and walked out of the room. Not long after Aggie left, Danny felt reality flooding back into his mind. Suddenly, he opened his eyes and looked around the room and called for the nurse.

Sara was in the hallway when she heard Danny shouting.

"Nurse! Nurse!"

The first thing that Sara thought was, "It can't. It's not possible!"

Dropping everything that she was doing at that time, she ran down the hall and into Danny's room. When Sara arrived at the room, she saw Danny sitting up in the bed with his eyes open, and her eyes were wide with surprise.

"You're back!" exclaimed Sara.

"Where is Aggie?" she asked.

"Aggie? Who is Aggie?" asked Danny.

"I…I am not sure who she is." replied Sara.

In her heart, Sara knew that the small elderly lady had performed some kind of miracle. Meanwhile, in the same town on a main street at about eight o'clock in the morning, a janitor was going about his daily duties of cleaning the recreation room at the local YMCA.

While sweeping the floor, he noticed a man passed out on the pool table with a whiskey bottle in his hand. The man was starting to wake up.And, when he did, he had no idea where he was. The man on the pool table sat up and looked around.When he saw the janitor he asked,

"Where am I?"

The janitor stopped sweeping and paused to think about what the man had just asked him. Then the janitor replied,

"You are nowhere, son. You are nowhere."

Printed in the United States
154110LV00002B/42/P

9 781438 989723